FOR DAD

(OCTOBER 27, 1943 - APRIL 27, 2021)

WEDDELL SEA
74 DEGREES SOUTH BY 52 DEGREES WEST
0200 HOURS

MIETTE
MIETTE

MAYDAY!
MAYDAY!

MAYDAY!
MAYDAY!

MAYDAY!
MAYDAY!
MICHEL!

THIS IS CAPTAIN MICHEL REVOY OF THE MIETTE RESEARCH VESSEL! DOES ANYONE READ? OVER?!

GZZZT
THHK
CHHK

WE HAVE TO GO NOW!

BLAST IT! THIS THING IS WORTHLESS!
CRACK

PAUL! GRAB WHAT YOU CAN!

REVOY

THWIP

JULES

LES

CRASH!
JULES
AAAGH!

JULES

GASP!
MICHEL!

THE SHIP IS ABOUT TO SINK!
IF WE WORK TOGETHER, WE CAN GET YOU OUT!

NNNNNGH!

I'M GONNA
GO GET HELP!
I'LL BE R—

JULES

...PAUL...
I'M NOT GOING
TO MAKE IT.
JULE

YULE
IT'S OUR LIFE'S WORK! TAKE IT, OR THIS IS ALL FOR NOTHING!

YOU NEED TO GO! TELL SOPHIA—

BWEEP
BWEEP
BWEEP

BWEEP

BWEEP
I CAN'T HEAR YOU!

BWEEP
BWEEP

QUA LAN
BWEEP
BWEEP

BWEEP BWEEP

BWEEP
BWEEP
BWEEP

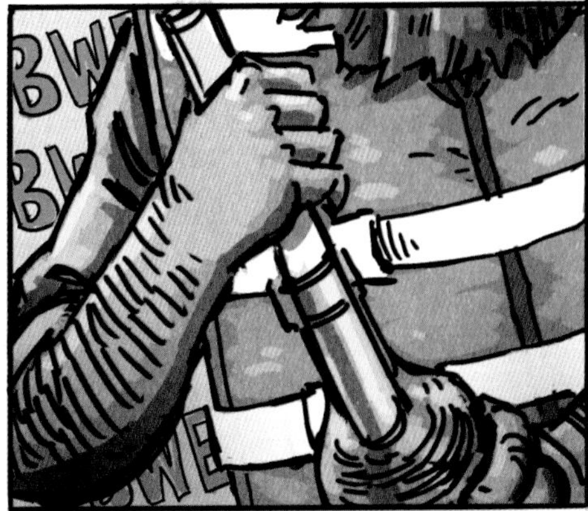

CRASH!
MICHEL! THE HULL HAS BEEN BREACHED!

PAUL! COME ON!
HUH?!

WE'VE GOT TO GO! THE SHIP WILL GO DOWN ANY MINUTE!
BUT HE'S STILL IN THERE! WE HAVE TO SAVE HIM!
WE'RE SORRY, PAUL, BUT THERE ISN'T ANY MORE TIME!

BWEE
MICHEL!
BWEEP
BWEEP
BWEEP
PAUL!
BWEEP
BWEE

HUH?!
LAND

...BRRR...
HUFF
HUFF
HUFF

HUFF
HUFF
CHATTER
CHATTER
CHATTER
GASP!
HUFF
HUFF

MMPH!!

PTHHHHHT!

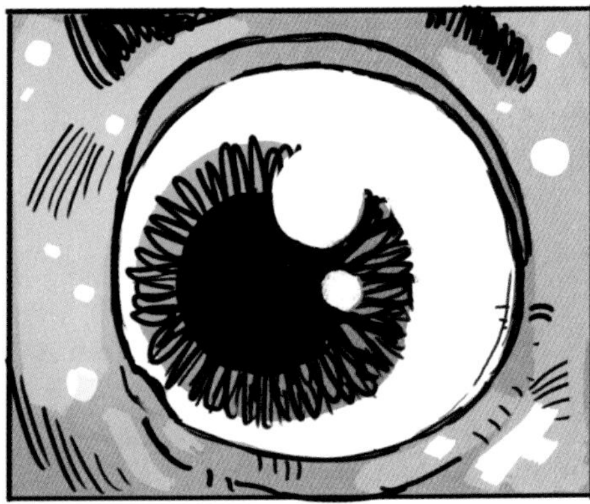

AQUALA

WE'RE SO SORRY, PAUL. HAD WE KNOWN MICHEL WAS TRAPPED, WE WOULD HAVE COME SOONER.

WE DID WHAT WE THOUGHT WAS RIGHT.

JULES

GUURK-URK-URK

GUURRRRRRK
MIETTE

MICHEL!

MICHEL!

THE AQUANAUT

A STORY BY

DAN SANTAT

An Imprint of
SCHOLASTIC

FIVE YEARS LATER
RIING RIING RIIING
8:30
YOU'VE REACHED PAUL AND SOPHIA, WE'RE NOT HOME RIGHT NOW, BUT PLEASE LEAVE A MESSAGE AT THE BEEP.
BEEP

UH, HI, SOPHIA, IT'S ME, MARTHA. I HOPE YOU'RE COMING TO SCHOOL TODAY. MRS. WEXLER WAS PRETTY TICKED OFF THAT YOU DIDN'T SHOW UP YESTERDAY...
OH NO!

LUNCH IN KITCHEN
ANOTHER FAILED TEST? WE NEED TO TALK
DON'T FORGET ABOUT THE SCIENCE FAIR ON FRIDAY. MRS. WEXLER SAYS YOU'LL HAVE TO TOTALLY ACE THE FAIR TO PASS THE CLASS.
Sophia
D-
OKAY, WELL, I'LL TALK TO YOU LATER.
FAMILY MEETING 8 PM

BRUSH
BRUSH
BRU

OM NOM NO
NOM N NO
NOM NO
NOM N

HAVE A GOOD DAY ♥
CLANK

MEANWHILE...
SAN DIEGO IS UP AHEAD 3,000 YARDS, CAPTAIN.

HOLD HER STEADY. MAN YOUR STATIONS.
AYE AYE!

HOLD ON, EVERYONE! ENTERING SPACE ON MY MARK!
3...2...1...

SPLASH

ANTONIO! STATUS REPORT!

THE HULL IS SECURE! CARLOS IS DIVERTING MORE POWER TO THE LEGS TO BEGIN WALKING!

STOMP
STOMP

STOMP

STOMP
MAMA! LOOK AT THE ROBOT!
WHAT IS THAT THING?
WHO IS THAT WEIRDO?
LOOK AT THAT!
WHOA! IT'S LIKE A SUPERHERO!
WHERE DID HE COME FROM?
IS THIS SOME SORT OF PRANK?
STOMP
STOMP

WHAT'S THAT THING?
WHO IS THAT GUY?
WHAT'S GOING ON OVER THERE?
WE'RE ATTRACTING TOO MUCH ATTENTION!
I'M HAVING A BAD FEELING ABOUT THIS.
WE'RE GONNA GET CAUGHT!

EXCUSE ME! YOUR DIVING SUIT LOOKS PRETTY OLD, AND I NEED TO MAKE SURE IT'S UP TO REGULATION.

A PERSON OF AUTHORITY! IT'S BEST YOU DO AS HE SAYS!
I AGREE.

EXCUSE ME? HELLO? DO YOU UNDERSTA—

WE'VE BEEN DISCOVERED!

TAKE EVASIVE ACTION!
SMACK

HEY!

CRASH!!
HEY!

WHAT THE?

SKREECH

DID WE LOSE THEM?!
I DON'T HEAR ANYTHING!
I DON'T KNOW!

LOOK AROUND THE CORNER!
OW! OKAY! RELAX! QUIT PUSHING ME!

WOOF
DID YOU HEAR SOMETHING?
WHAT WAS THAT?

GAH! WHAT IS IT?!
WOOF!

WHAAA! IT'S ATTACKING US!
WOOF!

I THINK THIS IS HOW AIR BREATHERS GREET EACH OTHER!

MAYBE IT CAN GIVE US DIRECTIONS TO GET TO AQUALAND!
DO I LOOK LIKE I SPEAK ITS LANGUAGE?!
WHOA...

CAPTAIN! STARBOARD SIDE!

WHOA.

FUN FOR THE ENTIRE FAMILY
AQUALAND
SAN DIEGO
SEAWARD EXIT
HEY, THERE'S DIRECTIONS ON THE BOTTOM!
WE'RE CLOSE! SEE?! I TOLD YOU!
IT'S MAGNIFICENT!

IT'S JUST LIKE IT SAID IN DR. REVOY'S JOURNAL. A PLACE TO KEEP ALL SEA CREATURES SAFE. IT'LL BE OUR SAFE HAVEN!
WE'RE ALMOST HOME!

MEANWHILE...
AHEM! MISS REVOY, CARE TO JOIN OUR DISCUSSION?!

I'M AWAKE! I'M AWAKE!
HA HA HA

IT WOULD BEHOOVE YOU TO PAY ATTENTION TO THE DETAILS ABOUT THE UPCOMING SCIENCE FAIR, CONSIDERING YOUR PAST TEST PERFORMANCES.

YOU'LL NEED TO DO SOMETHING PRETTY SPECIAL IN ORDER TO MAINTAIN A PASSING GRADE IN THIS CLASS.
YES, MRS. WEXLER.

NOW, LET'S GET BACK TO OUR DISCUSSION.

I'M SO SCREWED. I'M NOT EVEN READY FOR THIS PROJECT.
PSST HEY, SOPH...

WHILE YOU WERE SLEEPING, MRS. WEXLER WAS TALKING ABOUT EXTRA CREDIT. JUST SOMETHING THAT MAKES THE PRESENTATION MORE INTERESTING.

...REALLY?

HOMEWORK
MRS. WEXLER?

SIGH YES, SOPHIA. WHAT IS IT?
WORK

I WAS WONDERING IF I COULD BRING IN MY UNCLE TO HELP WITH MY PRESENTATION FOR EXTRA CREDIT.

GASP REALLY?!

UH, YEAH. HE'S BEEN REALLY HELPFUL DURING MY RESEARCH, AND I'M SURE HE WOULD BE HAPPY TO TALK MORE ABOUT OUR DATA.
THAT SOUNDS LIKE A WONDERFUL IDEA, SOPHIA. I LOVE YOUR INITIATIVE!

AND I WOULD THINK IT WOULD BE WORTH A NICE BONUS OF EXTRA CREDIT, AS WELL.

UNCLE PAUL, COULD YOU COME SPEAK AT MY SCIENCE FAIR?

COME ON. COME ON.
...

DING!
SURE!
YES!

SOPHIA!
SORRY!

LATER THAT AFTERNOON...

WELCOME TO AQUALAND
WELCOME TO AQUALAND
ADMISSION

WHOA.

SEVENTY-FIVE PERCENT OF OUR PLANET IS COVERED IN WATER. OUR OCEANS ARE AN ESSENTIAL SOURCE OF LIFE AND A DELICATE PART OF OUR ECOSYSTEM.

I'M DR. MICHEL REVOY, MARINE BIOLOGIST AND COFOUNDER OF AQUALAND!
AND I'M DR. PAUL REVOY!

WE'VE COLLECTED A WIDE VARIETY OF SEA LIFE FROM ALL OVER THE WORLD, WHICH ARE TO BE CARED FOR LIKE MEMBERS OF OUR OWN FAMILY.
WE HOPE YOU AND YOUR LOVED ONES WILL HAVE A GREAT TIME HERE AT OUR MARINE RESERVE.

AQUALAND! WHERE FAMILY COMES FIRST!

AAAAAAA
QUAT

UH, CAPTAIN.

WHERE ARE ALL THE SEA CREATURES?

I DON'T KNOW. THIS ISN'T WHAT I EXPECTED, EITHER.

LET'S REFER TO THE CAPTAIN'S JOURNAL.
REVOY

HMMM. THIS SEEMS TO BE THE RIGHT PLACE.
I JUST DON'T GET IT.

distribution
COEFFICIENT
MAYBE WE MADE A MISTAKE?

SKREEETCH...
WE NEED TO LOOK AROUND FOR CLUES.

OOF!

I'M SO SORRY, SIR!
I DIDN'T SEE YOU!
I APOLOGIZE!

AAAH!
WE'VE BEEN SPOTTED!

UHHHH...
WHO IS SHE? HOW LONG HAS SHE BEEN STANDING THERE?!
MAYBE SHE DIDN'T SEE US! JUST HOLD STILL!

UH...
ARE YOU OKAY?

WE NEED TO RUN AWAY!
STOP IT, JOBIM!

GET YOUR HANDS OFF THE CONTROLS!

SOPHIA, WHAT HAVE YOU GOTTEN YOURSELF INTO?

I'M SORRY AGAIN ABOUT BUMPING INTO YOU. MY MISTAKE!

GASP STOP!
WHAT?! WHAT IS IT?!
I KNOW WHO THAT GIRL IS!

JOBIM! THAT GIRL! IT'S HER!
HER?! HER WHO?!
THE GIRL IN REVOY'S JOURNAL!

WHAT?! ARE YOU SURE?!

YES! I'M POSITIVE! LET ME FIND IT!
FLIP FLIP FLIP FLIP

SEE?! HERE SHE IS!

REVOY USED HER PICTURE AS HIS BOOKMARK!
GASP FOLLOW HER!

AUTHORIZED
PERSONNEL
ONLY

GASP
THAT'S IT.
REVOY
MARINE
RESERVE

THAT'S
REVOY'S
OLD LAB!

OKAY,
CREW.

LET'S GO
INSIDE.

WOW! LOOK AT THIS PLACE!
THIS IS AMAZING!
WHERE DID THE GIRL GO?

CAN YOU BELIEVE THIS PLACE?
WE'LL NEVER HAVE TO WORRY ABOUT FOOD AGAIN.

GASP

THERE ARE OTHERS JUST LIKE ME!
I'VE NEVER SEEN OTHERS LIKE ME BEFORE!

IS THAT?!
YES! IT IS!

IT'S ANOTHER BLANKET OCTOPUS!
I'VE NEVER SEEN A MORE BEAUTIFUL CREATURE!

SEA TURTLE EGGS!
I CAN RAISE OTHERS LIKE ME!

WHAT IS THAT OVER THERE?
FOOD? I'M STARVING!
CARLOS! STOP!
AFTER SCHOOL SNACK - UNCLE PAUL

WHAT ARE YOU DOING?!
GASP! I NEED TO GET OUT OF THIS THING!

CARLOS! GET BACK IN HERE!
RELAX, CAPTAIN! I JUST WANT TO STRETCH MY TENTACLES.
WHAT IS THIS WEIRD MEAT?

LOOK AT ALL THIS STUFF. SPACE IS FASCINATING!

THIS PLACE IS A MESS.
YEAH, IT KIND OF SMELLS, TOO.

WHOA, CAPTAIN.
YOU HAVE TO SEE THIS...

WHOA! LOOK AT THIS, CAPTAIN!
AQUA

IT'S DR. REVOY!
MIETTE
AND THAT'S THE SHIP WE WERE ON!

AND THAT'S THE GIRL! COULD IT BE—
THE GIRL MUST BE DR. REVOY'S DAUGHTER! SHE COULD HELP US!
CAPTAIN!

I'VE HIT THE JACKPOT, CAPTAIN!
THERE'S FOOD HERE FOR ALL OF US!

CARLOS! WHAT ARE YOU DOING?! GET DOWN!
PLEASE! I JUST WANT ONE!

CRASH!

WH-WHO ARE YOU?

CRASH!

AAAAAAAAAAA

OH NO! WHAT DO WE DO?!
WE HAVE TO ESTABLISH COMMUNICATION! LET HER KNOW WE'RE FRIENDLY!

SLOWLY, SODAPOP. WE DON'T WANT TO SCARE HER OFF.

GASP
QUICK! BLOCK THE EXIT!

GASP

WE NEED TO CALM HER DOWN! LICK HER FACE!
AAAAAAAA

AAAAAAAAAA

CRASH!

GAH!

REVOY
CLUNK

GASP

...WHAT...?

...THIS IS MY DAD'S JOURNAL...
REVOY

WHO ARE YOU?
FIRST A

CLANK
GASP SOMEONE'S COMING!

QUICK! I'VE GOT TO HIDE YOU!
CLIMB INTO MY HANDS!

A DOLPHIN PETTING ZOO? AN ORCA SHOW?! THIS IS A MARINE RESERVE, NOT A CIRCUS! AQUALAND'S REPUTATION HAS BECOME A JOKE.
I DO APOLOGIZE, DR. REVOY, BUT I NEED YOUR FULL PARTICIPATION.

WHOOSH!
IF YOU WANT THIS FACILITY TO PROSPER, YOU MUST MEET THE INVESTORS AND TELL THEM WHAT THEY WANT TO HEAR.

THERE'S NO MONEY IN SAVING ENDANGERED SEA LIFE, DR. REVOY.
AND I'M NOT IN THIS FOR THE MONEY.

MAYBE THE FAULT IS IN YOUR RESEARCH, DR. REVOY. YOUR "JULES" EXHIBIT HAS COST AQUALAND A FORTUNE, AND IT HAS YET TO WORK OUT.

CAPTAIN, WHAT'S A "JULES"?
...I DON'T KNOW...

I SHOULD HAVE CANCELED THIS PROJECT YEARS AGO. BUT YOU BEGGED AND BEGGED—
HOW DARE YOU!

PAUL, LET ME BE BLUNT.
GET THEM INVESTED IN THE ORCA SHOW, OR I'M PULLING YOUR FUNDING.

I'M ALL YOU HAVE RIGHT NOW.

MR. LULA... I'M TRYING... PLEASE DON'T.
MY PATIENCE IS WEARING THIN.
NO MONEY.
NO JULES.
NO AQUALAND.

FINE...I'LL TALK TO THE INVESTORS...
THANKS...
"PARTNER."

WE SHOULD KEEP A LOW PROFILE WHILE WE'RE HERE.

EXIT
I HAVE A FEELING THIS WON'T BE THE LAST TIME WE SEE HIM.

HEY, KIDDO.

HOW WAS SCHOOL TODAY?

IT WAS OKAY, I GUESS. I CAME OVER TO TALK TO YOU ABOUT HELPING ME WITH MY SCIENCE PROJECT.

DARN IT! THAT'S RIGHT.
SOPHIA, I'M SORRY, BUT I DON'T KNOW IF I HAVE TIME TO HELP YOU WITH THAT NOW.

I WOULDN'T NEED TOO MUCH OF YOUR TIME. ONLY A COUPLE OF HOURS. I WAS IN TROUBLE WITH THIS ASSIGNMENT BEFORE. WITHOUT YOU, I'M PROBABLY GONNA FAIL.

MRS. WEXLER WILL UNDERSTAND. I'LL CALL HER.
JUST FORGET IT. I KNEW YOU WOULDN'T HELP.
YOU'RE ALWAYS TOO BUSY FOR ME.

SOPHIA, YOU HAVE TO UNDERSTAND. I PROMISED YOUR DAD THAT I WOULD PRESERVE OUR LIFE'S WORK.

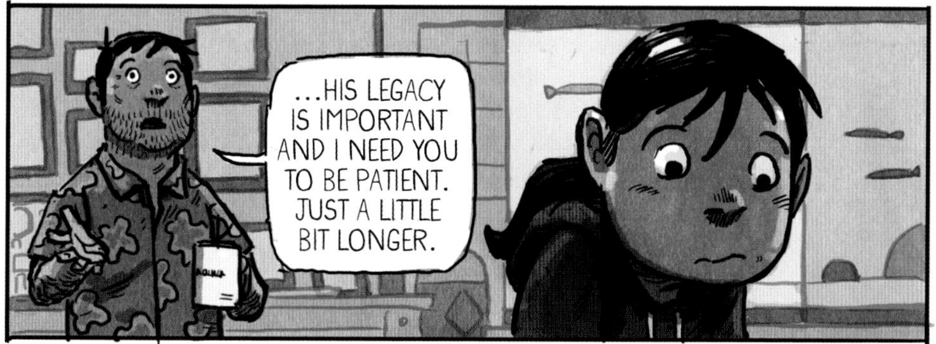
...HIS LEGACY IS IMPORTANT AND I NEED YOU TO BE PATIENT. JUST A LITTLE BIT LONGER.

CAN YOU DO THAT FOR ME?

OKAY, UNCLE PAUL.

I LOVE YOU.
I KNOW IT'S HARD.

I LOVE YOU, TOO, UNCLE PAUL.
AQUALAN

SQUIRT
I KNOW YOU'LL ACE THIS ASSIGNMENT.

YOU'RE A REVOY!

SIP

UGH.
GROSS.

I'M DOOMED. WHAT AM I GONNA DO FOR THE SCIENCE FAIR NOW?

JUST RELAX.
DO EVERYTHING I SAY AND NOD YOUR HEAD A LOT. GOT IT?
SCIENCE FAIR
SIGH I DON'T EVEN KNOW IF YOU CAN UNDERSTAND ME...
IT KINDA FEELS LIKE I'M TALKING TO A CAT...

...WEARING MY DAD'S OLD SUIT.

I REALLY HOPE THIS WORKS.

THIS ISN'T WHAT WE AGREED ON. WE'RE OUT IN THE OPEN FOR EVERYONE TO SEE!
WHAT DID YOU WANT ME TO DO, JOBIM? SHE GOT US TO AQUALAND! WE OWE HER!

UUUGH! I FEEL SICK!

WHAT'S WRONG WITH CARLOS?
STOMACHACHE. HE ATE TOO MUCH THIS MORNING.
KEEP AN EYE ON HIM! MAKE SURE HE STAYS OUT OF TROUBLE, AND CONCENTRATE ON ACTING LIKE AN UNCLE!

AND HERE WE HAVE MISS REVOY. SO NICE OF YOU TO JOIN US TODAY.

AND THIS MUST BE THE FAMOUS DR. PAUL REVOY! WHAT A HUGE HONOR IT IS TO HAVE YOU AT OUR SCHOOL TODAY, AND IN SUCH A LOVELY COSTUME!

...
SAY "HI," UNCLE PAUL.

SHOULD I LICK HER FACE?
IT'S WORTH A SHOT.

UNCLE PAUL!

WHAT DO YOU THINK YOU'RE DOING? KNOCK IT OFF!

COULD YOU GIVE US JUST A MOMENT, PLEASE?

WHAT AM I GONNA DO? MY HANDS ARE SHAKING AND I'M WORRIED AND—

WHA? WHAT ARE YOU—

OH, OKAY...

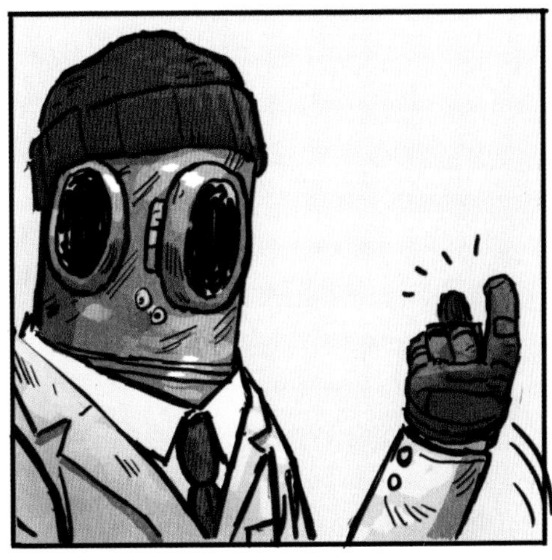

...

I DON'T KNOW WHAT THAT WAS, BUT IT HELPED. THANKS.

I'M READY TO BEGIN, MRS. WEXLER.

HUH? OH, YES.
WHERE WERE WE?

WE EXPECT WONDERFUL THINGS FROM YOU TODAY.

YES, THANK YOU, MRS. WEXLER. TODAY, I'M HERE TO DO A PRESENTATION ON SEA MONKEYS.

DID YOU SAY SEA MONKEYS?

YES, THEY'RE ACTUALLY QUITE FASCINA—

...OH NO...

CARLOS, WHAT DID YOU DO?!
IT WASN'T ME, CAPTAIN! I JUST SNACKED ON A FEW BRINE SHRIMP! I NEVER SAW ANY SEA MONKEYS!

YOU IDIOT! BRINE SHRIMP ARE SEA MONKEYS!

YOU HAVE TO FIX THIS, CARLOS! YOU MADE THIS MESS, AND NOW YOU HAVE TO FIX IT!

GRK

UH, SOPHIA? IS THERE A PROBLEM WITH YOUR UNCLE?

HE'S FINE. HE DIDN'T HAVE HIS COFFEE THIS MORNING, SO HE'S KIND OF CRANKY.

...I SEE...

YOU'RE GOING TO SIT THERE AND YOU'RE GOING TO BE THE MOST AMAZING SCIENCE FAIR PROJECT EVER! DO YOU HEAR ME?!

KLANK

IS EVERYTHING OKAY, SOPHIA?

FINE.
NEVER BETTER.

PSSST LISTEN. WE'RE GONNA HAVE TO WING IT. FOLLOW MY LEAD.

HERE GOES NOTHING.

MRS. WEXLER!
HONORED JUDGES!
SLIGHT CHANGE OF PLANS!
ALLOW ME TO INTRODUCE YOU TO MY SPECIAL SCIENCE FAIR PROJECT ON...

?

THE OCTOPUS!

ER, I MEAN...

THE DUMBO OCTOPUS!

CONTINUE.

WELL, UH, THE DUMBO OCTOPUS CAN DO ALL SORTS OF COOL STUFF...

...LIKE...
COIL
PLAN

WHOOSH!

THEY CAN GLOW IN THE DARK THROUGH BIOLUMINESCENCE!

SCRIBBLE
SCRIBBLE
SCRIBBLE
CAT OBESITY
CHONK
SOLAR SYSTE

WHAT ELSE?

THIS IS ONE THING I'M SURE CARLOS WILL BE GOOD AT.

SOPHIA

PLOOSH
CHIPS

UGH. WHAT IS THIS WEIRD MEAT? I CAN'T—

SPLASH!

YOU DO IT, OR I SWEAR I'M GOING TO MAKE YOU SORRY!

SPLASH!
HEH HEH. THE DUMBO OCTOPUS HAS AN AMAZING APPETITE FOR ALL SORTS OF FOOD.

UGH... THIS ISN'T GOOD.

I'M GONNA BE SICK!

URK!

GET BACK IN THERE AND FINISH THAT TURKEY SANDWICH!
YOUR CAPTAIN GAVE YOU A DIRECT ORDER!
HE'S GONNA LOSE IT!

I'M GONNA BE SICK!

SMACK
AAAAH!
GURGLE

BAAAARF!
AAAAAAAAAAA
I'M SO GETTING AN F.

THREE MONTHS LATER
MY DAD AND I USED TO SWAP SEASHELLS BEFORE HE WOULD LEAVE ON A RESEARCH TRIP.
SHELLS $1.00

SOMETIMES I STILL FIND SHELLS FOR HIM WHEN I'M WALKING ON THE BEACH.

I GUESS OLD HABITS ARE HARD TO BREAK.

SEE THIS?

THIS WAS THE LAST SHELL MY DAD GAVE ME.

$5.00
WE SHOULD GET GOING.

EXCUSE ME, SIR!

YOU HAVE TO PAY FOR THAT. IT'S FIVE DOLLARS.
I DON'T SET THE PRICES. I JUST SELL THE MERCHANDISE.
POSTCARDS $1.00
SALES

HOLY SMOKES!

IS THIS REAL GOLD?!

SIR, I DON'T HAVE ENOUGH CHANGE IN THE REGISTER FOR THIS!
KEEP THE CHANGE! THANKS!
SALE

HA! HA!
HA! HA! HA!
HA!

WHEW! THAT WAS A CLOSE ONE!

NOW WHERE ARE—
...OH NO...

NOT HERE.
WE SHOULD GO.

WELCOME TO OUR NEW KILLER WHALE SHOW HERE AT AQUALAND!
IF YOU ARE SEATED IN THE FIRST EIGHT ROWS, YOU WILL GET WET!

WHAT IS THIS PLACE?

HOW DOES HER TONGUE FEEL, LITTLE LADY?
IT'S SQUISHY!

ORCAS ARE HIGHLY INTELLIGENT CREATURES.

BUT WHEN SHE DOESN'T BEHAVE, WE IGNORE HER UNTIL SHE COOPERATES!

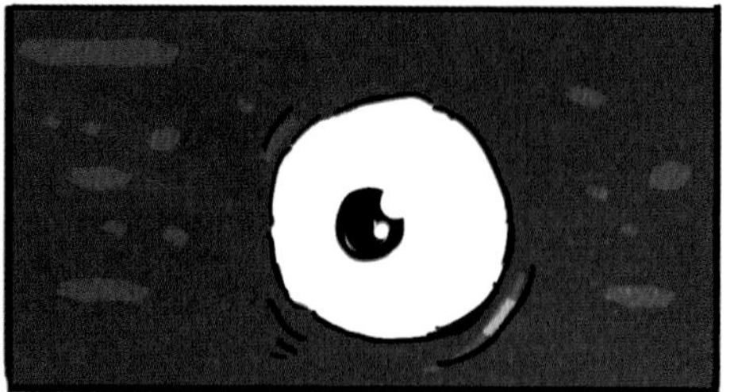

A

SHE'S SCARED.

101

MY DAD NEVER WOULD HAVE AGREED TO ANY OF THIS. IT'S MR. LULA. MY UNCLE DOES ANYTHING HE SAYS AS LONG AS HE PAYS FOR HIS RESEARCH.
HE WORKS ALL DAY AND NIGHT ON HIS SUPER SECRET RESEARCH PROJECT THAT HE AND MY DAD STARTED TOGETHER YEARS AGO.

OOF!

HEY! WHERE ARE YOU?

?!
SNACKS

PETTING POOL

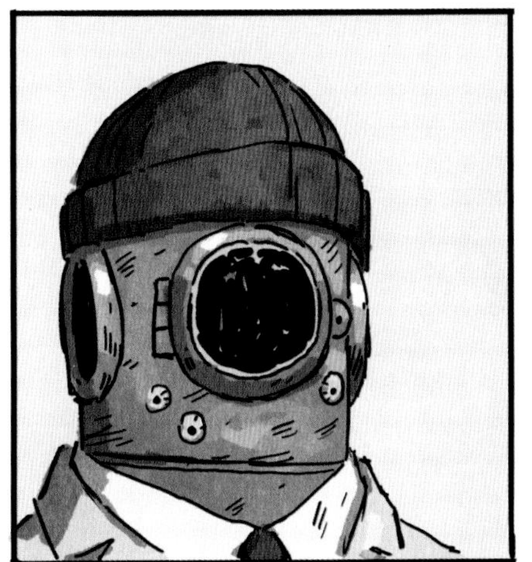

STAND NEXT TO HIM!

IT'S FINE, HONEY. HE WORKS HERE.
I DON'T WANT TO.

YOU DON'T MIND, DO YOU?
WE'D LIKE A PHOTO, TOO!

GET IN THERE!
NO!
WE'RE NEXT!

THERE YOU ARE! I WAS LOOKING EVERYWHERE FOR YOU!

SORRY, FOLKS, THERE WILL BE NO PHOTOS RIGHT NOW. THIS CHARACTER IS GOING ON HIS BREAK!
7

UH-OH.

I THINK WE SHOULD LIE LOW FOR A BIT.

QUICK! IN HERE! IT'S OFF-LIMITS TO EVERYONE ELSE.
PARDON OUR DUST
A NEW EXHIBIT IS COMING
AQUALAND

THIS IS ONE OF THE MOST ADVANCED TANKS IN THE WORLD TODAY.

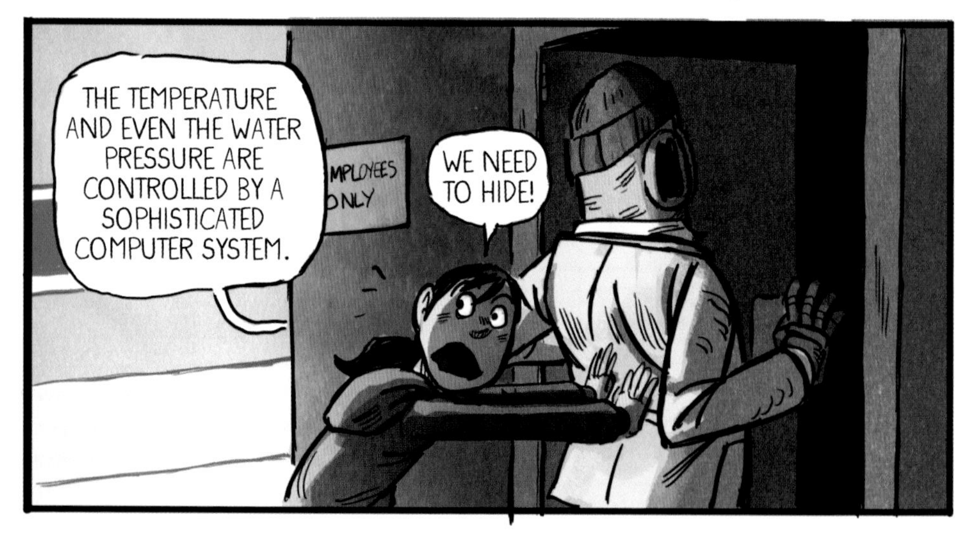
THE TEMPERATURE AND EVEN THE WATER PRESSURE ARE CONTROLLED BY A SOPHISTICATED COMPUTER SYSTEM.
WE NEED TO HIDE!

THE CONTROL ROOM IS LOCATED ON THE FLOOR RIGHT ABOVE US.

WHY IS THE WATER SO MURKY, DR. REVOY?

WE'VE HAD DIFFICULTIES WITH THE SPECIMEN SINCE IT'S BEEN HERE.
IT WAS BORN IN CAPTIVITY, AND WE KNOW VERY LITTLE ABOUT IT.

IT'S THE FIRST OF ITS KIND TO EVER BE HOUSED IN A MAN-MADE FACILITY, BUT I ASSURE YOU, I CAN HANDLE IT.

FOLLOW ME AND I'LL SHOW YOU THE CONTROL ROOM.

WHEW. THAT WAS CLOSE. I THINK WE SHOULD GET BACK TO THE RESEARCH FACILITY AND LIE LOW FOR—

—A WHILE...
EP

DEEP
HEY! WHAT ARE YOU DOING?

THE CREATURE FROM THE DEEP
WE NEED TO GET BACK—

MONSTER!

WHAT'S GOING ON?! WHAT'S WRONG?!

SKRITCH
SKRITCH
SKRITCH
WHAT DO I DO?!

SOMEBODY HELP!

OKAY, SON, YOU CAN
OPEN YOUR EYES NOW...

WHOA!

DID ALL THIS STUFF COME FROM SPACE?
YES.
HOW DID ALL THIS STUFF END UP DOWN HERE?
HUMANS DUMP THINGS INTO THE OCEAN WHEN THEY DON'T WANT THEM ANYMORE.

MUCH OF IT ISN'T VERY GOOD FOR THE OCEAN. BUT SOMETIMES YOU FIND SOME UNIQUE THINGS...

LIKE THIS.
I THINK THIS WAS USED TO HELP HUMANS MIGRATE LONG DISTANCES.

WHAT DOES UNIQUE MEAN?
IT'S SOMETHING SPECIAL. ONE OF A KIND.

LIKE MAMA?

YES. MAMA WAS UNIQUE.

WOW. IT'S AMAZING TO THINK THAT HUMANS USED TO USE THIS THING.

HEY, LOOK OVER THERE!

WHAT IS IT?
THIS THING WAS USED TO HOLD LIQUIDS FOR HUMANS TO DRINK.
IT MIGHT BE A GREAT NEW SHELL FOR YOU TO REPLACE THE SMALL ONE YOU'RE WEARING.

OOH! IT'S AMAZING.

HAVE YOU EVER BEEN TO SPACE BEFORE?
I HAVE.
WHAT'S IT LIKE?

IMAGINE A PLACE WHERE NO WATER IS AROUND YOU. THAT'S WHY IT'S CALLED SPACE. IT'S FILLED WITH ALL SORTS OF AMAZING CREATURES AND PLANTS.

ARE THERE MONSTERS UP IN SPACE?
NO. NOT ONES THAT I'VE EVER SEEN.
I WANT TO GO SOMEDAY. WE SHOULD LIVE THERE!

ROOOAAR!

WHAT WAS THAT?!

I DON'T KNOW...

GASP
SHHHHH!!!

ROOOAAAAR
AAAH!

MONSTER! MONSTER! MONST-

DON'T MOVE! QUIET! YOU HAVE TO BE QUIET, BOY!
M-MONSTER... ...MONSTER...

WHAT DO WE DO WITH BAD THOUGHTS IN OUR HEAD?

...WE PULL THEM OUT...

AND THROW THEM AWAY.

NOW CALM DOWN AND CLOSE YOUR EYES.

WE'RE SAFE HERE.

WE'RE OKAY.

WE'RE SAFE.

HOURS LATER
I DON'T HEAR ANYTHING...

I THINK IT'S GONE.

I THINK WE'RE SAFE!

...

THERE'S NOTHING
TO BE AFRAID OF.

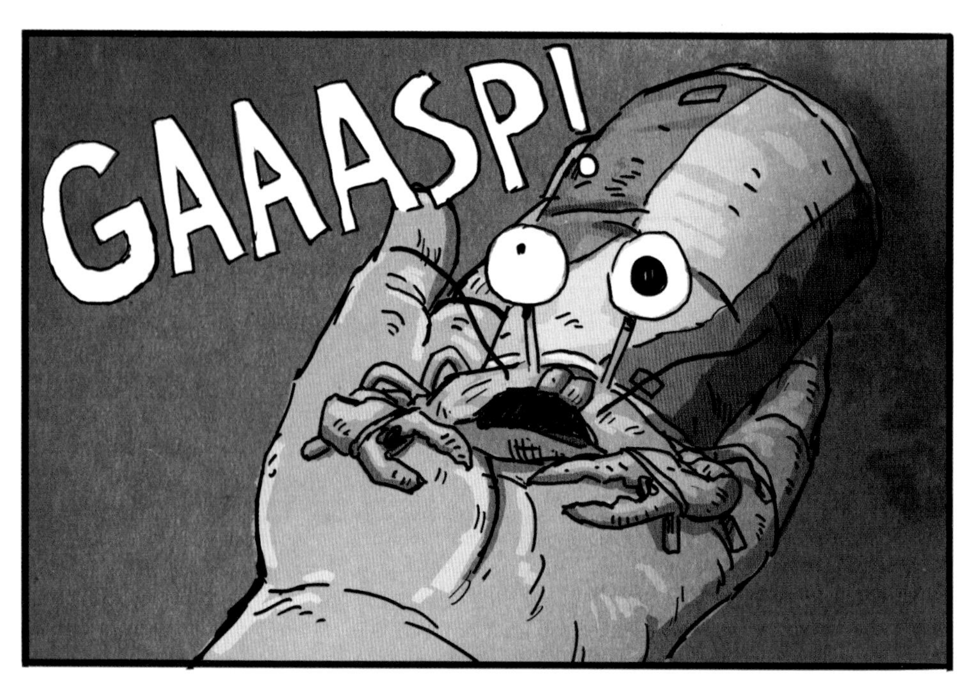
GAAASP!

YOU DID IT! HE'S OKAY!

I THINK HE'S GONNA BE FINE.
BUT, SOPHIA...

YOU HAVE A LOT OF EXPLAINING TO DO...

SLAM!

OKAY. LOOKS LIKE THE COAST IS CLEAR.

CLOSE THE DOOR BEHIND YOU.
OKAY.

WHAT'S GOING ON?
I THINK WE'VE JUST BEEN DISCOVERED.

AQUALAND

AQUALAND

CAVE
AQUALAND

AQUALA

YUCK.

AQUAL

OKAY. TALK. WHAT IS THIS THING?
AQUALA

I FOUND THEM WANDERING AROUND YOUR OFFICE...
HE WAS MY SCIENCE FAIR PROJECT...

WAIT. WHAT?!
AQUALA!

WHY—
ARE —
YOU—
HERE?!
AQUAL

THEY UNDERSTAND US. YOU DON'T NEED TO SHOUT AT THEM.

YOU REALIZE HOW RIDICULOUS THIS ALL SOUNDS, RIGHT? I MEAN, HOW DID THEY END UP HERE?

THEY FOUND US USING THIS.

MICHEL'S JOURNAL?!

I...I THOUGHT THIS WAS GONE FOR GOOD.
REVOY

I THINK THEY CAME HERE BECAUSE THEY THOUGHT IT WOULD BE SAFE FOR THEM.

THEY CAME FROM THE MIETTE... THAT WAS FIVE YEARS AGO.

EXCUSE US ONE MINUTE.

THEY CAN'T STAY HERE. THEY HAVE TO GO.
WHAT? WHY?!

THIS IS PROBABLY ONE OF THE MOST SIGNIFICANT DISCOVERIES IN SCIENCE, AND IT'S STANDING RIGHT OVER THERE!

MR. LULA DOESN'T KNOW, AND I WANT TO KEEP IT THAT WAY!
NO ONE NEEDS TO KNOW. IF WE KEEP IT A SECRET, THEY CAN BE SAFE AND HAPPY HERE!

I FOUND IT CONVULSING ON THE FLOOR OF MY EXHIBIT! YOU TOOK IT TO YOUR SCHOOL AS A SCIENCE PROJECT! HOW IS THAT SAFE?!

YOU DITCHED ME WHEN I NEEDED HELP! I HAD TO DO SOMETHING!

IMAGINE IF IT HAS ANOTHER PROBLEM. WHAT WILL YOU DO? IF MR. LULA FINDS OUT, WE'LL NEVER SEE IT AGAIN.

WE CAN TAKE CARE OF THEM. THEY NEED US.

NO.

IT'S TOO RISKY.

ALL I HEAR FROM YOU IS HOW YOU'RE WORKING DAY AND NIGHT ON YOUR SPECIAL PROJECT BECAUSE IT WILL SAVE AQUALAND. YOU SAY IT'S WHAT DAD WOULD HAVE WANTED.
I NEVER SEE YOU ANYMORE. I'VE SPENT MORE TIME WITH THEM IN THE LAST MONTH THAN I HAVE WITH YOU IN THE LAST FEW YEARS.

THEY'VE BEEN MORE OF A FAMILY TO ME THAN YOU HAVE LATELY.

SOPHIA...I...

I NEED THEM. I NEED SOMEONE, AND THEY NEED US. YOU CAN OBSESS ABOUT WORK ALL YOU WANT, BUT I SWEAR, IF YOU MAKE THEM LEAVE...

I'M GONNA RUN SO FAR AWAY THAT YOU'LL NEVER FIND ME.

PLEASE... HELP THEM.

OKAY.

OKAY, SOPHIA. THEY STAY.

THAT MAN, MR. LULA, DOESN'T CARE WHAT GOES ON IN THE RESEARCH LAB. I PROMISE I CAN KEEP YOU SAFE HERE, BUT YOU CAN NEVER LEAVE THE FACILITY. DO YOU UNDERSTAND?

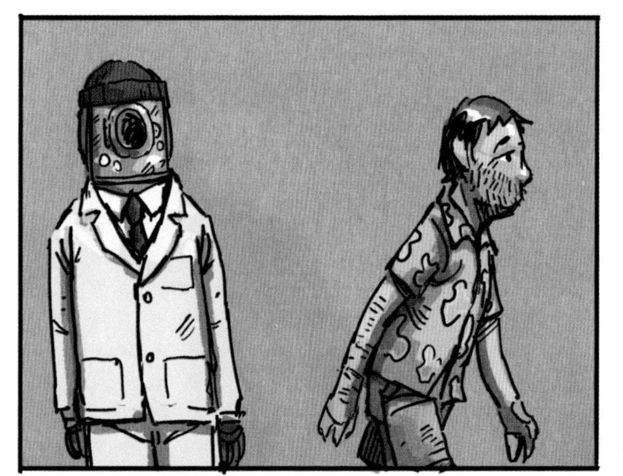

EXIT

SLAM!

PROMISE YOU WON'T LEAVE THE LAB ANYMORE.
YEAH, TELL US YOU'RE FINISHED WANDERING AROUND.

I CAN'T...
THERE'S SOMETHING I NEED TO SHOW ALL OF YOU.

!
SNAP!

WHEW! JUST A SQUIRREL.

HMMMM.
DON'T REMEMBER SEEING THAT STATUE BEFORE.

I DON'T HAVE A GOOD FEELING ABOUT THIS, CAPTAIN.

WE'RE GONNA GET CAUGHT.
SHHH. NOT IF WE DO THIS QUIETLY.

REMIND ME AGAIN WHY WE'RE RISKING OUR NECKS FOR A KILLER WHALE?

YOU DON'T HAVE TO DO THIS IF YOU DON'T WANT TO.

LET'S JUST GET THIS OVER WITH QUICKLY.

SNACKS
OCEANA

MOMENTS LATER
AQUALAND
THE POOL IS EMPTY. WHERE IS THE ORCA?
THEY KEEP HER IN A SMALLER POOL WHEN SHE'S NOT PERFORMING. IT'S OVER HERE.

AUTHORIZED PERSONNEL ONLY

AUTHORIZED PERSONNEL ONLY

DOES ANYONE KNOW HOW TO DRIVE A TRUCK?
AQUALAND
2BZK131

IF WE CAN DRIVE THE AQUANAUT, HOW HARD CAN A TRUCK BE?

YOU GUYS FIGURE OUT THE TRUCK AND CRANE.
I'LL GO TALK TO THE ORCA.

WHO ARE YOU?
I'M A FRIEND. I'M HERE TO FREE YOU.
WHAT DO YOU KNOW OF MY PAIN?

BECAUSE I COULD SEE IT IN YOUR EYES.

I BROUGHT HELP. WE'RE GETTING YOU OUT OF HERE.

BEEP BEEP
WHAT'S THAT SOUND?

BEEP BEEP BEEP
CALIFORNIA
2BZK131
WHOA!

SO "R" MEANS GO BACKWARD. GOT IT!

MEANWHILE...
HMMMM...OPERATING A CRANE SHOULDN'T BE TOO HARD...

WHICH LEVER DO I PULL?

OH WELL, HERE GOES NOTHIN'!
CLANK

CLANK!

SPLASH!

I DID IT!

GET INTO THE NET, AND WE'LL HOIST YOU UP!

I HOPE YOU KNOW WHAT YOU'RE DOING.

YOU'LL BE FINE. TRUST US!

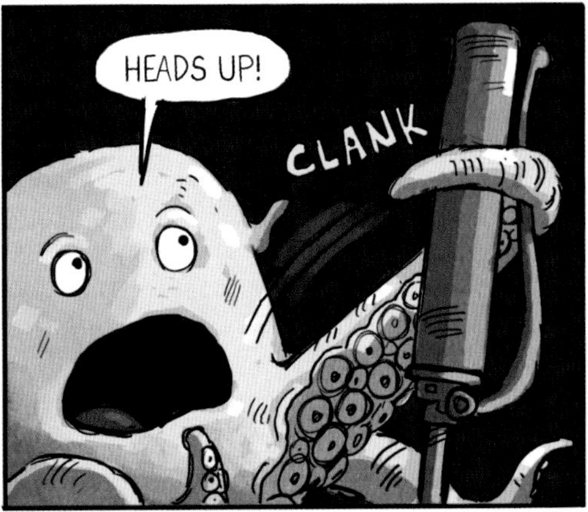
HEADS UP!
CLANK

WOOSH!

CAREFUL WITH HER!
SORRY!

IT'LL BE A MIRACLE IF WE CAN PULL THIS OFF.

GET ME DOWN FROM—

CLANK!
—HERE.

SPLASH!
AQUALAND

ARE YOU OKAY?!
I'M FINE. LET'S GO!

WE BETTER GET A MOVE ON, CAPTAIN!

COME ON, CARLOS!
COMING!

VROOOM!!
CALIFORNIA
2BZK131

HUH?

HEAD FOR THE DOCK! WE'LL FREE THE ORCA INTO THE OCEAN!

JOBIM!
I KNOW! I'M STILL FIGURING THIS OUT!

LET'S TRY ONE OF THESE NUMBERS!
1 3 R
2 4

HERE WE GO!

CRASH!

KEEP IT UP! WE'RE LOSING THEM!

HUFF
HUFF
HUFF

I THINK WE'RE FAR ENOUGH FROM THE FACILITY!

NOW TO DROP OFF THE ORCA!
SAN DIEGO HARBOR
AQUALAND

SCREEEEE

EEEEEEEE
WHOA!
SLAP!

WHAT ARE YOU DOING?!
EEEEETCH!
SLOW DOWN, JOBIM!

STOP THE TRUCK!

I DON'T KNOW HOW TO STOP!

WHAT?!

BRACE FOR IMPACT!

VROOOOM!

AWOOOOOOOOOO
SPLOOSH!

WE NEED TO GET OUT OF HERE!
THE DOOR IS STUCK!

CRUNCH

HANG ON! WE'LL GET YOU TO THE SURFACE!

I MUST LEAVE YOU HERE.
I CAN DO NO MORE THAN THAT.

THANK YOU. YOU'VE DONE MORE THAN ENOUGH.

NO. I SHOULD BE THANKING YOU.
YOU SAVED MY LIFE, AND I AM FOREVER GRATEFUL.

FAREWELL,
MY FRIENDS.

WELL...

WHAT DO
WE DO NOW,
CAPTAIN?

WE SEE WHERE
THE TIDE TAKES US.

WHOOOSH

WHOOOOSHHHH

I'M SORRY I GOT YOU ALL INTO THIS MESS.

YOU DID THE RIGHT THING, CAPTAIN.
WE'RE IN THIS TOGETHER.

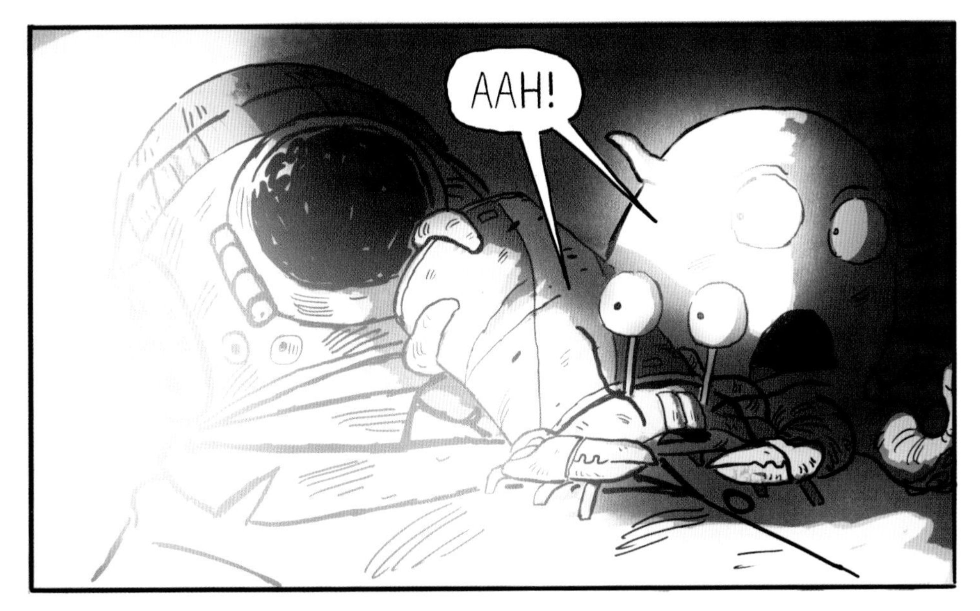
AAH!

WHAT ARE YOU DOING HERE? I TOLD YOU TO STAY IN THE LAB!

IT'S DR. REVOY!

HOW DID YOU GET OUT HERE?!

AWOOOOOOOOOOOO
...OH NO...

...THAT WAS MY WHALE...

GOOD MORNING! IT'S 8 A.M. AND HERE ARE THE MORNING HEADLINES.
A BREAK-IN OCCURRED AT THE AQUALAND MARINE RESERVE LAST NIGHT.
CORKY, THE FAMOUS AQUALAND KILLER WHALE, WAS RELEASED OUT TO SEA AROUND 3 A.M. LAST NIGHT.

LOCAL AUTHORITIES FOUND A TANKER TRUCK OFF THE SAN DIEGO PIER—
8:01

OH NO!

GASP UNCLE PAUL? WHAT ARE THEY DOING HERE?!

THEY HAD THE HAREBRAINED IDEA OF FREEING THE ORCA! I FOUND THEM WASHED UP ON THE BEACH WITH A BROKEN POWER LINE IN THEIR GUT AND BROUGHT THEM BACK HERE TO FIX IT.

BUT HOW ARE WE GOING TO GET THEM BACK INTO THE RESERVE?
SOPHIA...

THEY CAN'T STAY. IT ISN'T SAFE ANYMORE.

THUMP
THUMP
THUMP
REVOY! OPEN UP!

SOPHIA, GET THEM OUT OF HERE! GO OUT THE BACK, AND I'LL DISTRACT THEM!

AND YOU...

YOU HAVE TO LEAVE.

GO TO THE SEA AND NEVER COME BACK.
EVER.

COME ON, REVOY! WE KNOW YOU'RE IN THERE!

OH NO! THEY FOUND US!

GO. NOW.
FOLLOW ME! THIS WAY!

PAUL! THIS IS YOUR LAST—
BAM BAM BAM

CLICK
I WAS JUST MAKING TEA.
COME IN, PLEASE.

I DON'T KNOW WHO YOU THINK YOU ARE, BUT YOU HAVE SOME NERVE!
I DON'T KNOW WHAT YOU'RE TALKING ABOUT.

THE KILLER WHALE GOES MISSING THE DAY AFTER THE INVESTORS MET WITH YOU. I KNOW YOU STOLE THAT WHALE.
YOU KNOW HOW MUCH THIS WILL COST ME? NOT TO MENTION THE PROPERTY DAMAGE!

YOU'RE MISTAKEN! I WOULD NEVER DO ANYTHING LIKE THAT, MR. LULA!

MEANWHILE...
COME ON! WE'VE GOT TO GET OUT OF HERE!

WAIT.
I CAN'T LET UNCLE PAUL TAKE THE BLAME FOR ALL THIS.

STOP KIDDING AROUND, PAUL. I KNOW YOU HATED HAVING THAT WHALE AT THE FACILITY, SO YOU FREED IT YOURSELF.
I COULD HAVE YOU SENT TO PRISON. YOU WOULDN'T WANT THAT FOR YOUR NIECE, NOW, WOULD YOU?
YOU HAVE NO PROOF.

GASP

WE FOUND THIS ON THE BEACH.
AQUALAND
PAUL REVOY
IT WAS ME.

SOPHIA?! WHAT ARE YOU DOING HERE?!

I STOLE MY UNCLE'S ID AND FREED THE WHALE. IF ANYONE SHOULD BE PUNISHED, IT SHOULD BE ME.

SOPHIA, DON'T DO THIS. I'M BEGGING YOU.
I HAVE TO DO THIS.

IT'S THE RIGHT THING TO DO.

THIS IS MY FAULT.

THEIR FAMILY IS GOING TO BE BROKEN APART BECAUSE OF ME.

BUT WE CAN'T STAY HERE.
WHERE WILL WE GO?
THE SEA IS OUR ONLY OPTION.

I CAN'T LET YOU BE PUNISHED FOR MY ACTIONS.

CAPTAIN...
YOU KNOW I'M RIGHT.

I ORDER YOU TO ABANDON SHIP.

HA HA HA HA
HA HA

WE ONLY CALL YOU CAPTAIN BECAUSE THIS WHOLE THING WAS YOUR IDEA.
BUT WE ALL AGREED TO BE EQUAL PARTNERS IN ALL OUR DECISIONS.

AND AFTER ALL THESE YEARS TOGETHER, WE'RE LIKE A FAMILY. AND LIKE THE REVOYS SAY...

FAMILY COMES FIRST.

CLICK

?
!
CREEEAK

WHAT ARE YOU DOING BACK HERE?!

WHO IS THIS MAN?

...

FASCINATING.

THESE SEA CREATURES ARE MANNING THIS SUIT ON THEIR OWN?

THIS COULD MAKE ME A FORTUNE.

NO, MR. LULA! YOU CAN'T TAKE THEM! THEY'RE NOT PUPPETS FOR YOU TO MAKE MONEY OFF OF!

HA HA HA HA HA HA

YOU THINK THIS IS UP TO YOU? I CAN STILL HAVE YOU THROWN IN JAIL!

CLACK!

HUH?

NO! DO YOU KNOW WHAT THIS MAN WILL DO TO YOU?!
WHY ARE YOU GOING WITH HIM?!

HE KNOWS WHAT'S GOOD FOR HIM. IN FACT, I DON'T THINK I'LL NEED YOU ANYMORE, DR. REVOY.

WHAT HAPPENS TO ALL MY RESEARCH?! WHAT HAPPENS TO MY SQUID?
THAT THING HAS BEEN A DRAIN ON MY WALLET FOR YEARS NOW.
YOU'RE DONE, DR. REVOY.

YOU CAN KISS ALL OF THIS GOODBYE.

NOW, COME WITH ME.

?

WHAT'S GOING ON?

I SAID COME HERE NOW!

DID YOU HEAR ME?!

HA HA HA

SO THAT'S HOW WE'RE PLAYING IT, HUH? OKAY. FINE.

IF YOU SUPERVISE THIS CREATURE, THEN I'LL MAKE SURE YOU KEEP YOUR JOB.
IS THAT A DEAL?

...AND MY SQUID.

FINE.
AND YOUR SQUID.

DO YOU MIND IF I HAVE A WORD ALONE WITH IT?

FINE.
TEN MINUTES.
NO FUNNY BUSINESS.

SIGH

?

WHAT THE?

SQUIRT
AQUALAND

AQUALAND

AGAVE NECTAR. I HATE THE STUFF.
ALWAYS HAVE.
AQUALAN

MY BROTHER USED TO DO IT, AND HE MADE ME TRY IT.
IT'S A HABIT NOW BECAUSE IT REMINDS ME OF HIM.
I'M AFRAID THAT IF I STOP, I'LL FORGET HIM.

IT'S UNSETTLING TO SEE THIS SUIT WALKING AROUND. IT WAS ALL WE COULD AFFORD AT THE TIME.

IT'S LIKE I'M TALKING TO A GHOST.

POP!

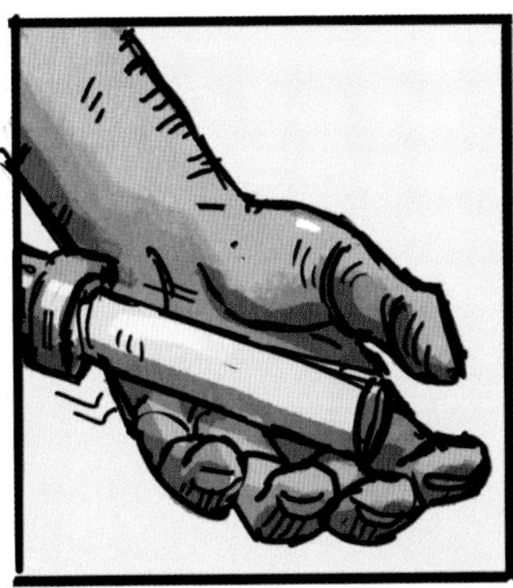

TAKE CARE
OF
SOPHIA

...I NEVER HAD A CHANCE TO SAY GOODBYE...

SIX MONTHS LATER
THE AQUANAUT
9TH WONDER OF THE WORLD
GOOD EVENING, IT'S 7 P.M. NOW IT'S TIME FOR THE LOCAL NEWS HEADLINES.
WORLD-FAMOUS MARINE BIOLOGIST DR. PAUL REVOY WILL BE MAKING HIS FIRST PUBLIC APPEARANCE IN FIVE YEARS.

TODAY HE IS REVEALING WHAT IS ANTICIPATED AS THE BIGGEST SCIENTIFIC DISCOVERY OF THE CENTURY.
THE AQUANAUT
A SUIT MANNED BY SEA CREATURES!

MEANWHILE...
GOOD. THE SEAL ON THIS SUIT IS SOLID...

EXCUSE ME! PLEASE DON'T STAND SO CLOSE TO THE SUIT.

SORRY, I DIDN'T MEAN TO SOUND RUDE, BUT THESE ARE VERY SENSITIVE CREATURES, AND I NEED TO MAKE SURE EVERYTHING IS PERFECT.

SLAM
PAUL! TODAY'S THE BIG DAY! IT FEELS ELECTRIC OUT THERE!
I LOVE THE NEW SUIT ON THE CREATURE!

HOW DOES IT MOVE?
HELLO? ANYTHING IN THERE?

WHOA! WHO ARE THESE PEOPLE!?
THEY'RE NEW INVESTORS!
THIS EVENT IS SURE TO BE A HIT! AFTER TONIGHT, WE'RE GONNA BE RICH!

FOLKS, PLEASE, IF YOU DON'T MIND, I NEED TO CHECK ITS VITALS BEFORE THE SHOW STARTS.
A

YES! OF COURSE! WE SHOULD GET OUT OF YOUR WAY!

WHAT DOES IT EAT?
DOES IT SLEEP?
WE WILL GIVE YOU ANSWERS!

BUT FOR NOW, I PROMISE YOU THAT IT WILL BE EXTRAORDINARY.
SLAM

SIGH

YOU KNOW WHAT TO DO.

OKAY...

HERE WE GO.

PAUL, YOU'RE ON IN TWO MINUTES!

JUST RELAX AND FOLLOW MY LEAD.
A

AND NOW I'D LIKE TO INTRODUCE YOU TO THE ONE... THE ONLY... DR. PAUL REVOY!

THANK YOU, EVERYONE! HOW ARE YOU ALL DOING THIS EVENING?!
WELCOME TO AQUALAND! I'M DR. PAUL REVOY!
HOORAY!
YOU'RE THE BEST!
CLAP
CLAP
WE LOVE YOU, PAUL!
CLAP
CLAP

WOW! IF I KNEW YOU WERE GOING TO GIVE ME SUCH A WARM WELCOME, I WOULD HAVE COME OUT SOONER!

HA HA
HA
HA
HA
HA
HA
HA

I KNOW WHY YOU'RE ALL HERE, AND I'M PLEASED AND HONORED TO SHARE THIS AMAZING DISCOVERY WITH ALL OF YOU IN THE AUDIENCE AND THE MILLIONS OF YOU WATCHING AT HOME!

SO, WITHOUT FURTHER ADO, ALLOW ME TO INTRODUCE...
THE AQUANAUT!

OOH!
LOOK AT THAT!
WOW!

AMAZING!
COOL!

TRIP

WHAM!

CLINK
CLANK

OH NO.

WHAT'S GOING ON?!
IS THIS A JOKE?
HE'S A FAKE!
GASP

OH NO.

REVOY!

WHAT HAVE YOU DONE?! WHERE IS IT?!

WHERE IS THE CREATURE?!

ALAND
BAM! BAM! BAM!

WHO COULD THIS POSSIBLY—

—BE?

AAAH!

WHO ARE YOU?!
WHAT DO YOU WANT?!

GASP

IT'S YOU!

YOU GOT AWAY! BUT HOW?!

DAD'S JOURNAL?

GASP THERE'S AN ESCAPE PLAN WRITTEN IN HERE!
STOP RIGHT THERE!

YOU HAVE TO STEP ASIDE!

NO! YOU STAY AWAY!

LITTLE GIRL, I'M WARNING YOU!
I'M NOT LETTING YOU TAKE THEM!

WHACK!

WHA?!
CLUNK!

WHAT JUST HAPPENED?

CLANG

CLANG
CLANG

CAPTAIN!
YOU ESCAPED!
WHERE'S DR. REVOY?
NO TIME TO EXPLAIN!

WE NEED TO GATHER ALL THE SEA CREATURES OUT OF ALL THE TANKS AND LOAD THEM INTO THE AQUANAUT! WE'RE ALL GETTING OUT OF HERE!

ATTENTION ALL SECURITY! BE ON THE LOOKOUT FOR A MAN IN A DIVING SUIT COSTUME!

QUICK! MY UNCLE HAS A PLAN, AND WE NEED TO GO!

GET IN YOUR OUTFIT! YOU NEED TO GET OUT OF YOUR DISGUISE!

MEANWHILE...
I'M RUNNING OUT OF PATIENCE WITH YOU, DR. REVOY.
WHERE IS THE AQUANAUT?

DO YOU REALIZE WHAT YOU'VE DONE?! YOU MADE US LOOK LIKE FRAUDS! WE'RE RUINED! AQUALAND IS THROUGH!

YOU'RE RUINED, MR. LULA. NOT ME.
YOU'RE JUST AN INVESTOR.

?
I'M A MARINE BIOLOGIST WITH YEARS OF CREDENTIALS.

HOW DARE YOU!!

I'M STILL THE WORLD-FAMOUS DR. REVOY.
INVESTORS COME TO SPEAK WITH ME—

—REMEMBER?

THAT THING IS NEVER GETTING OUT OF THE PARK! I HAVE EVERY EXIT COVERED, AND YOU CAN KISS YOUR PRECIOUS SQUID GOODBYE!

I'M GOING TO RELISH THE MOMENT WHEN I CAN FLUSH IT OUT TO SEA FROM THAT USELESS TANK.

WAIT.

THAT'S THE ONLY WAY LEFT OUT OF THE PARK...

...

ALL REMAINING SECURITY TO THE SQUID EXHIBIT NOW!!!

ROGER, WE HEAR YOU LOUD AND CLEAR!

MAN, HE'S A GROUCH.

WE SHOULD SPLIT UP.
I'LL GO THIS WAY. YOU GO THE OTHER WAY.
PARDON OUR DUST
A NEW EXHIBIT IS COMING
AQUALAND

THE CREATURE FROM THE DEEP

THIS IS THE ONLY PLAN WE HAVE! TRUST ME, I'M TERRIFIED, BUT I HAVE FAITH IN DR. REVOY.

OPERATIONS
WHOA.

I THINK WE'RE HERE.

OKAY, THERE IS A WATER VALVE. WE JUST NEED TO OPEN THE VALVE, LET THE SQUID SWIM OUT, AND THEN YOU JUMP IN AFTERWARD AND LEAVE THE SAME WAY.
WE JUST NEED TO FIND THE BUTTON.
CAUTION

ENGINE ROOM IS THIS WAY!
OH NO! THEY'RE COMING!

TRY TO HOLD THEM OFF!

WHAM!

THERE'RE TOO MANY OF THEM!
WE DON'T HAVE ENOUGH POWER TO HOLD THEM ALL OFF!

THEY'RE COMING IN!

HOLD ON, EVERYONE!

SHOVE!
SNAG!
RIP!

SHHH
SLIP!
SLIP!
SQUISH
CLUNK

THERE'S A BREACH IN THE HULL!
SHHHHH

ANTONIO, SEE WHAT YOU CAN DO!

I'M ON IT, CAPTAIN!

GOTCHA!

YOU'RE WORTH
A LOT TO ME!!!

AND YOU'RE NOT
GETTING AWAY!!

WE'RE STUCK!

I'M ON IT!

SMAK!

THWIP!
GAAAH!

HOLD ON, CARLOS!
SLIP!

I'M SHUTTING THE DOOR!

WAIT! PULL ME IN!
NOOOO!!!

SLAM!

CAPTAIN!!

OH NO!

IS HE OKAY?

CARLOS! HOW ARE YOU? HOW IS YOUR TENTACLE?

IT HURTS, BUT I'M FINE... MY BODY WILL GROW A NEW ONE.

CLAMP!

WHEW!

ANTONIO! STATUS REPORT!

THE TEAR IS SIGNIFICANT, BUT I THINK OUR REPAIR WILL HOLD FOR NOW!

I FOUND THE BUTTON!

VALVE
RELEAS

BEEEP!
WHA? WHY ISN'T IT WORKING?

OH NO.

THE SQUID IS BLOCKING THE VALVE WITH ITS BODY. IT'S BLOCKING THE WAY OUT!
WHAT DO WE DO?!
VALVE 1:OPEN

THAT THING IS STILL IN THERE! WE CAN'T RISK IT!

WE HAVE TO! IT'S OUR ONLY CHANCE TO GET OUT!
I AGREE! WE CAN'T STAY HERE!

I WANT THAT DOOR DOWN NOW!

BAM!
OH NO!

LIVE OR DIE, WE STICK TOGETHER!
BRACE YOURSELVES! WE'RE GOING IN!

WHERE ARE YOU GOING?!

FIRE
SMASH!

YOU'RE STILL GOING IN?!
WAIT FOR ME!

HOLD ON! THERE'S ONE MORE THING!

UNCLE PAUL LEFT THIS FOR YOU.

I HOPE THIS WORKS.

I KNOW YOU'RE SCARED, SO I WANTED YOU TO HAVE THIS.

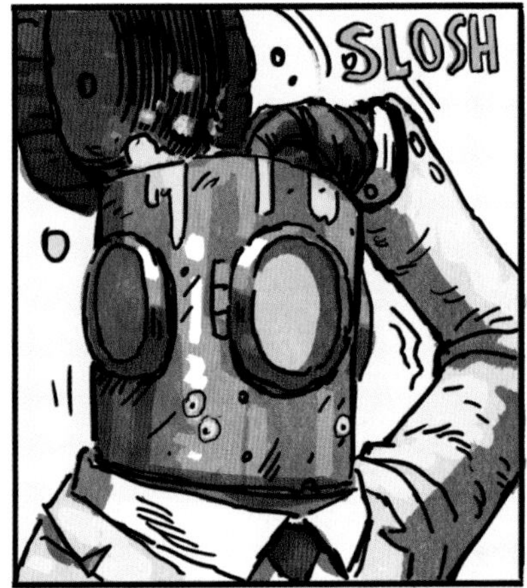
SLOSH

GOODBYE...

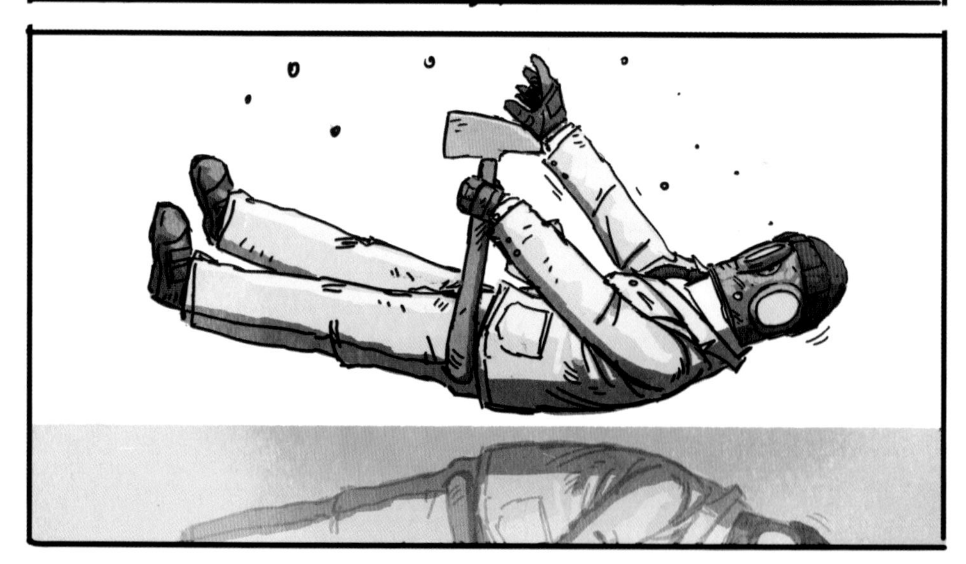

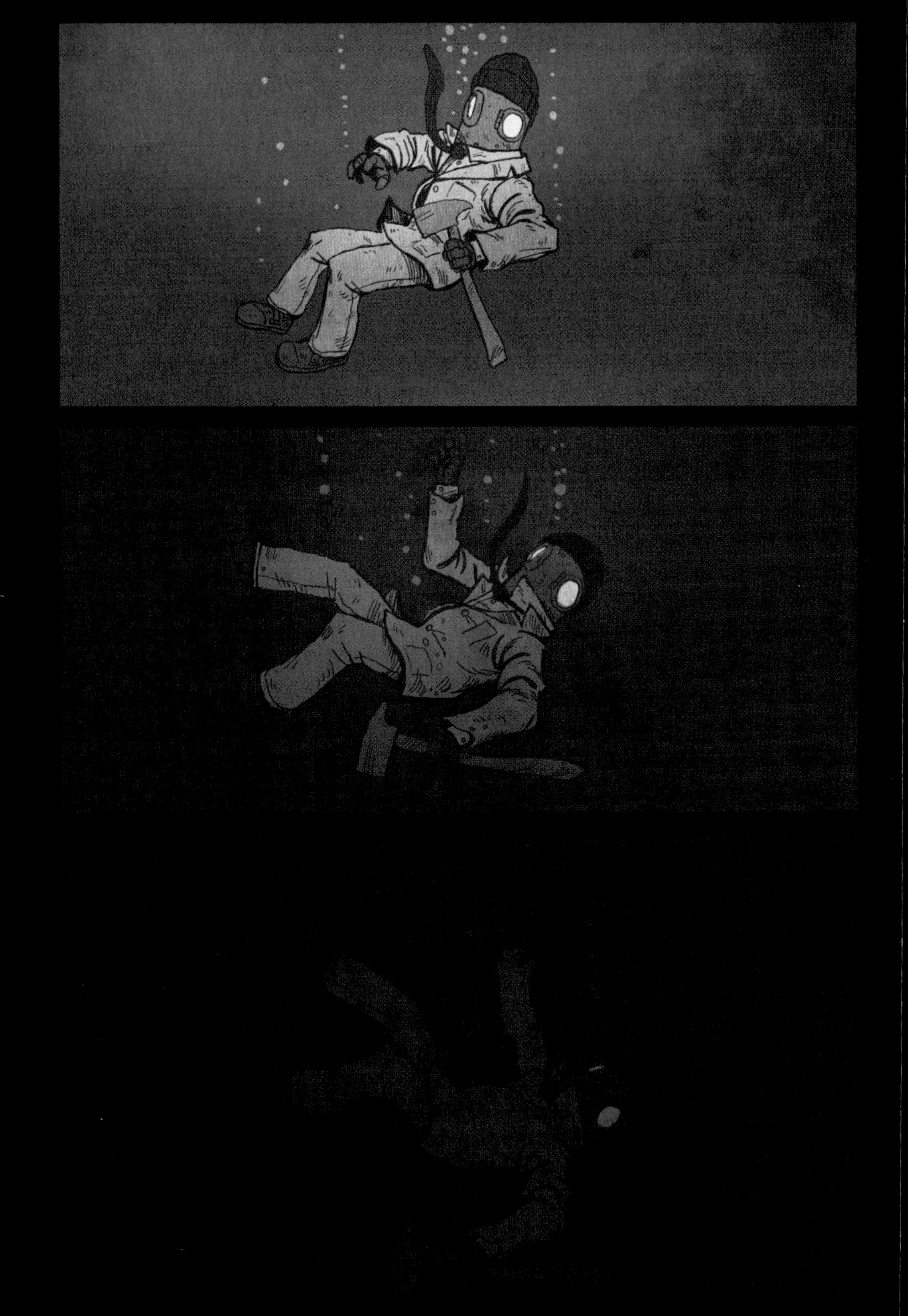

HUFF
HUFF
HUFF
HUFF

HUFF
HUFF
HUFF
SHAKE
SHAKE
SHAKE

SNAP

CALM DOWN, SODAPOP.
RATTLE

IT'S OKAY. WE'RE HERE WITH YOU.
JUST RELAX.

WHA?!

GAAAH!

WE'RE SITTING DUCKS OUT HERE, SODAPOP! WHAT DO WE DO?!

GASP

IT JUST BROKE THAT AXE LIKE IT WAS A TWIG!

GAAAH!

THWIP!

THE SQUID IS STARTING TO CONSTRICT!

POK
POK
POK

BARBS ARE BREACHING THE HULL!

BLACK STUFF IS SEEPING IN!
DON'T BE FRIGHTENED! COME WITH ME!

CAPTAIN! WE'RE RUNNING OUT OF POWER!

CAPTAIN! INK IS FILLING IN THE ENTIRE CABIN!
CAPTAIN! IT'S GETTING CROWDED IN HERE!

CAPTAIN! THE SHIP'S FALLING APART! WHAT DO WE DO?!
CAPTAIN!
CAPTAIN!
CAPTAIN!
CAPTAIN!
CAPTAIN!

CAPTAIN!

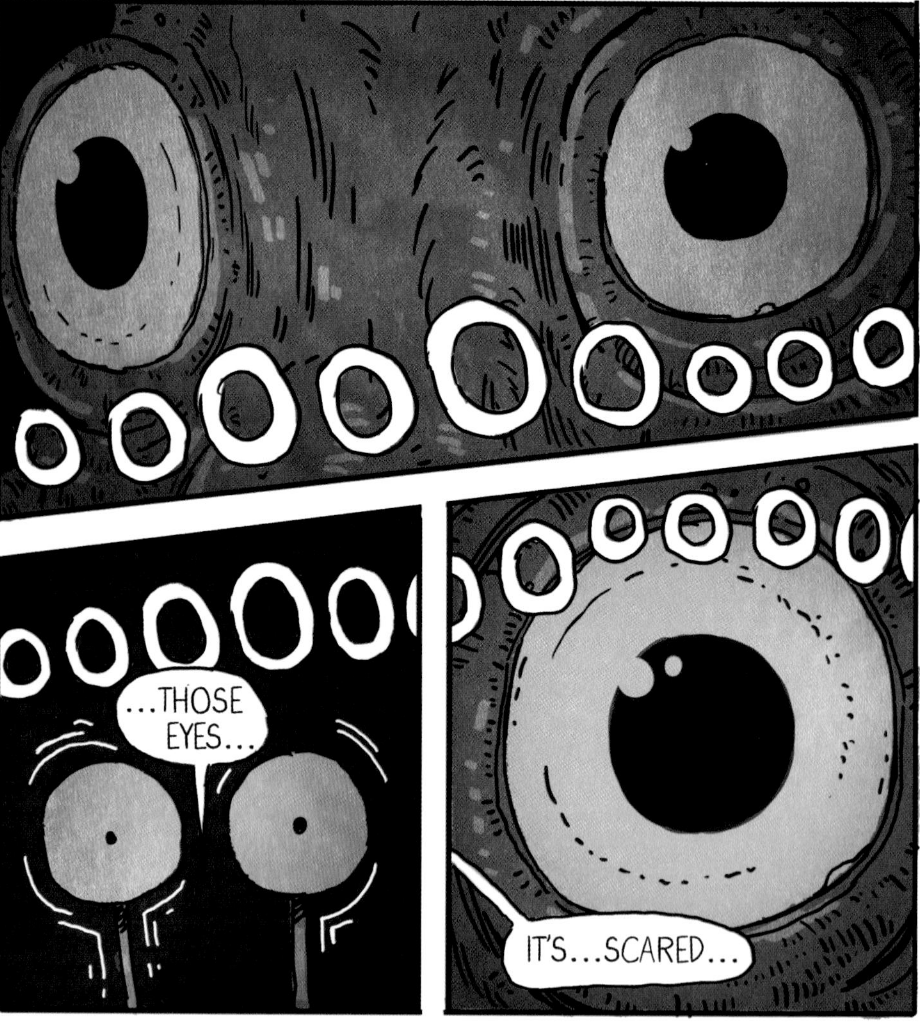
...THOSE EYES...
IT'S...SCARED...

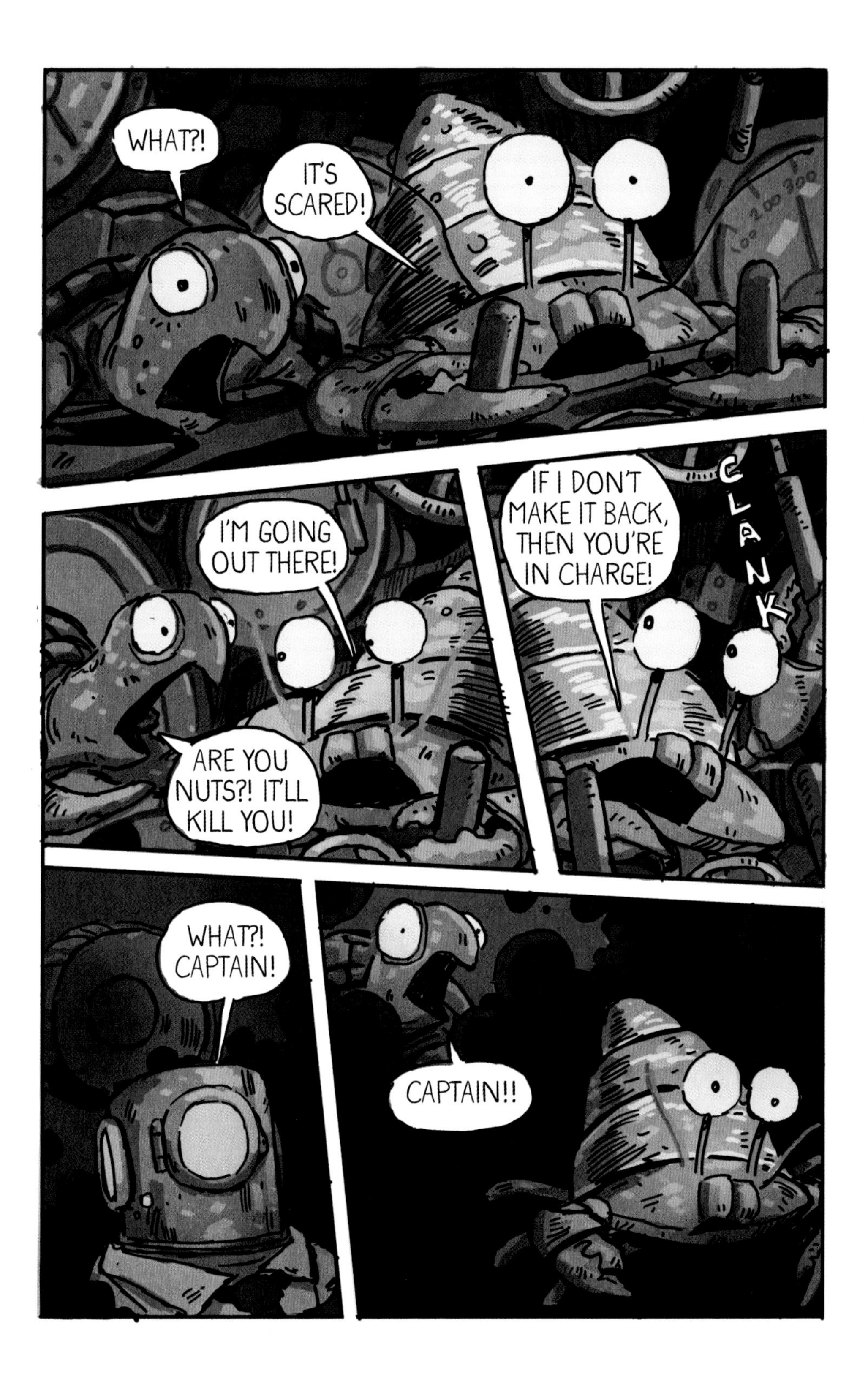
WHAT?!
IT'S SCARED!
I'M GOING OUT THERE!
ARE YOU NUTS?! IT'LL KILL YOU!
IF I DON'T MAKE IT BACK, THEN YOU'RE IN CHARGE!
CLANK
WHAT?! CAPTAIN!
CAPTAIN!!

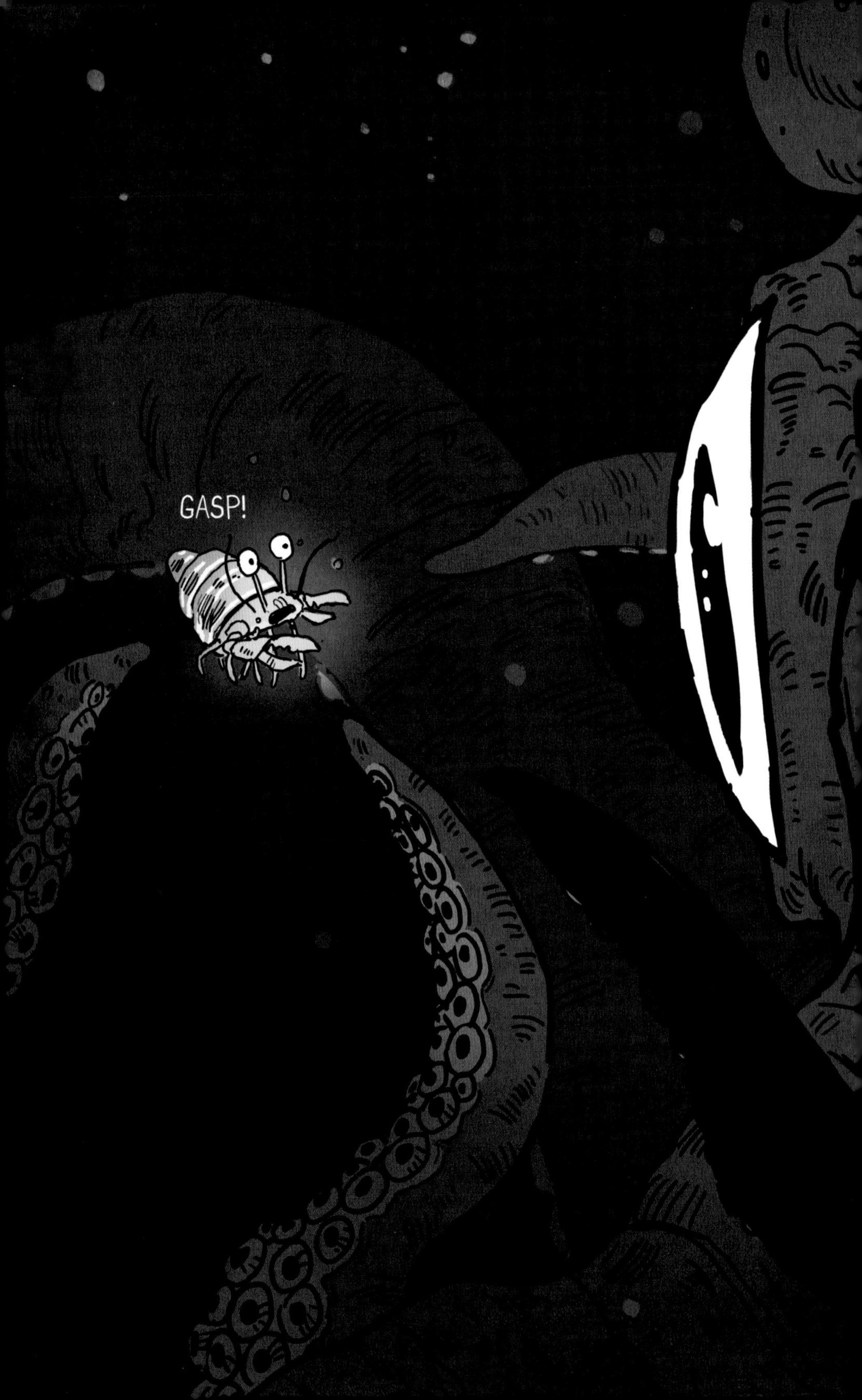
GASP!

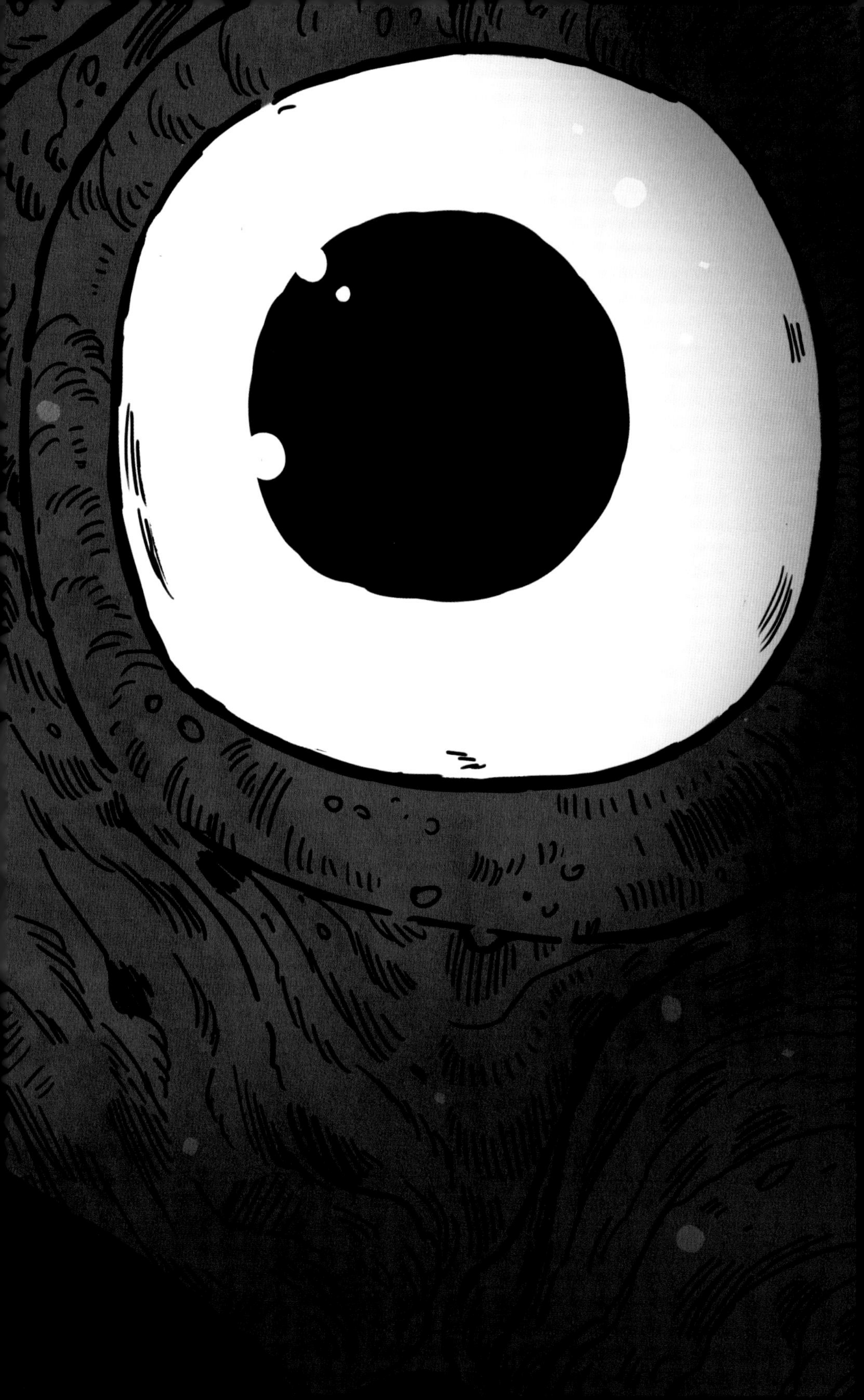

TAKE MY CLAW. I'LL SHOW YOU THE WAY.

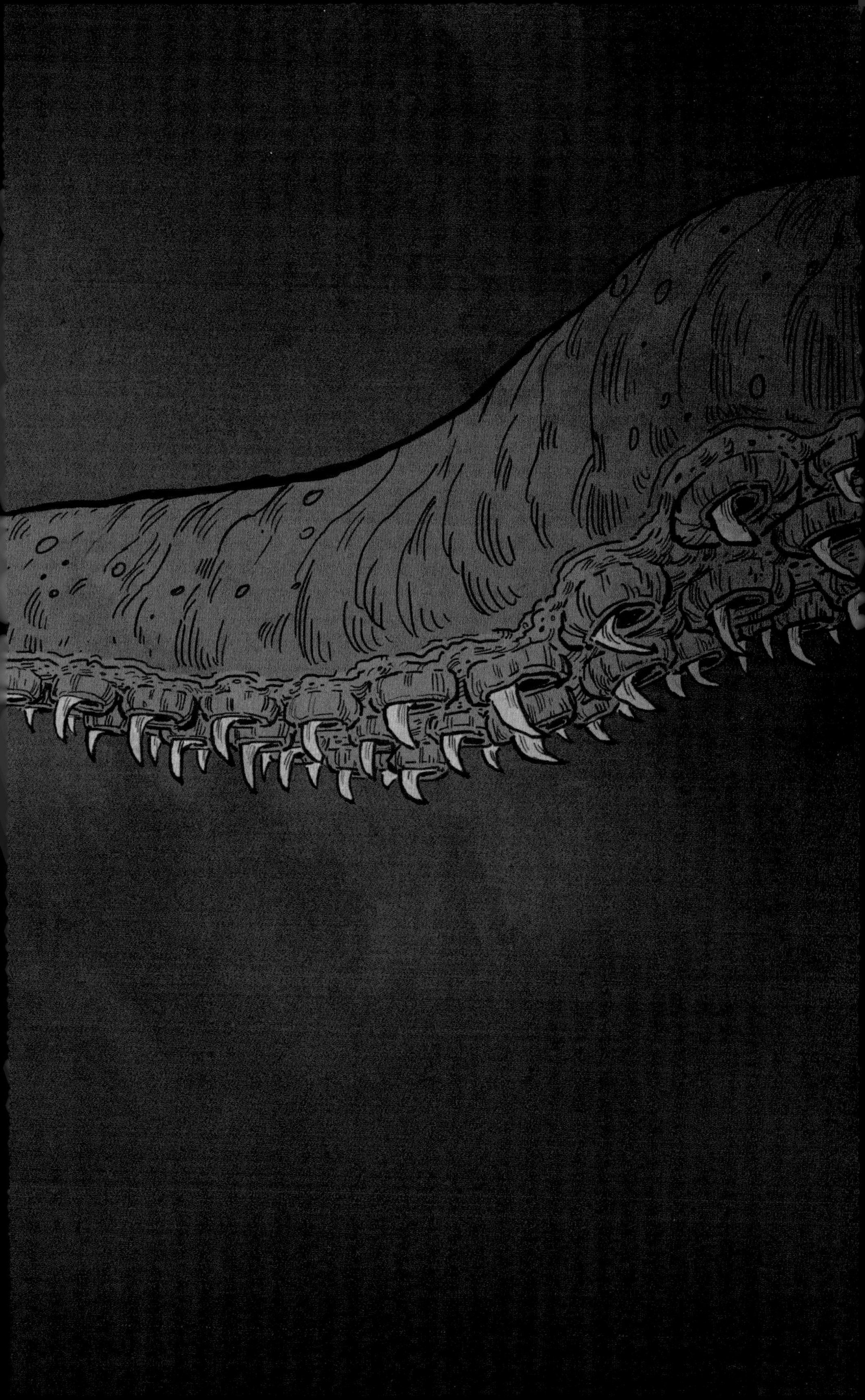

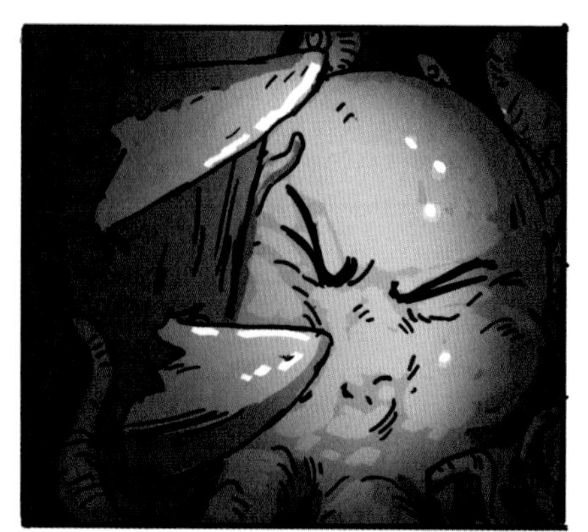

YOU DID IT, SODAPOP.

WE'RE FREE.

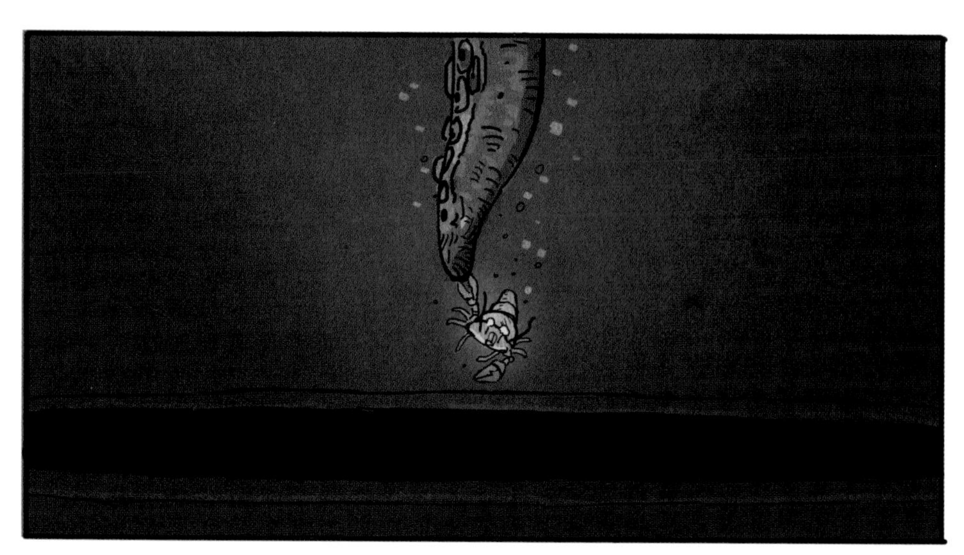

SAN DIEGO, CALIFORNIA

SIX MONTHS LATER

AQUALAND
NCE
GREETINGS. THIS IS DR. PAUL REVOY.
CLOSED
CLOSED
TO ALL OF YOU OUT THERE LISTENING TO THIS MESSAGE, I'M SAD TO SAY THAT AQUALAND IS CLOSING ITS DOORS FOR GOOD.

SOLD
GRIFFITH REALTY
555-8329
SINCE THE LOSS OF MY BROTHER, MICHEL, OUR FAMILY HAS UNDERGONE MANY PERSONAL CHANGES.
REVOY

THE LOSS OF MY BROTHER LEFT A HUGE HOLE IN MY HEART. AQUALAND WAS OUR HOME, AND I TRIED HARD TO PRESERVE IT.
SO MUCH SO THAT IT CONSUMED ME.

BUT I LEARNED THAT HOME ISN'T A PLACE. IT'S THE PEOPLE AROUND YOU.

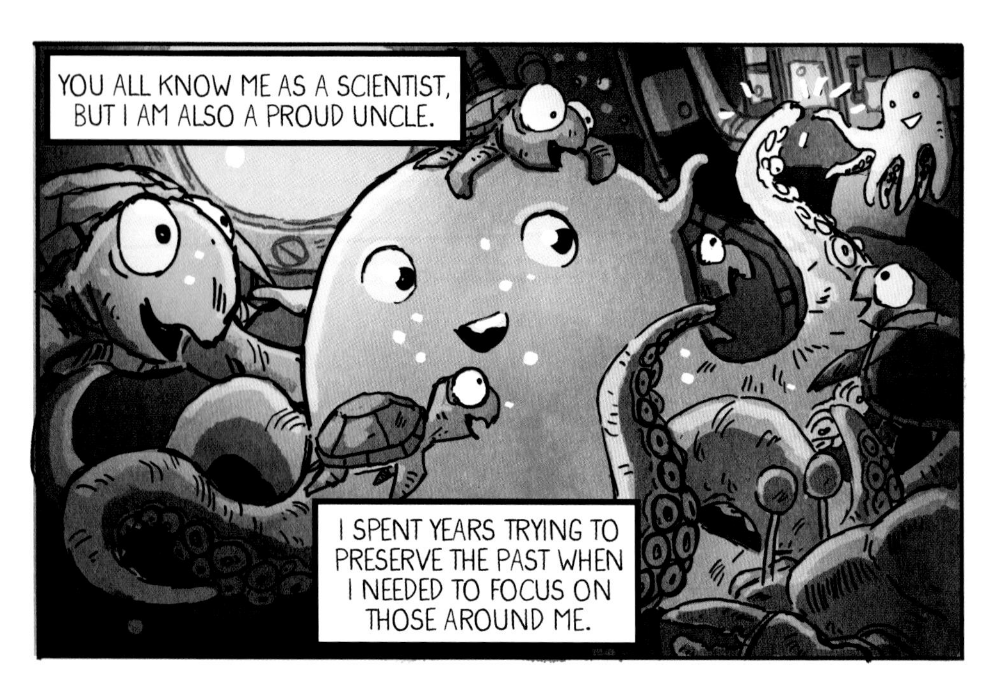
YOU ALL KNOW ME AS A SCIENTIST, BUT I AM ALSO A PROUD UNCLE.
I SPENT YEARS TRYING TO PRESERVE THE PAST WHEN I NEEDED TO FOCUS ON THOSE AROUND ME.

THERE'S NO GREATER PAIN THAN LOSING A LOVED ONE. IT CHANGES YOU IN WAYS YOU MAY NOT BE PREPARED FOR. THE THOUGHT OF BEING ALONE IN A VAST WORLD CAN SEEM QUITE OVERWHELMING.
BUT WITH THE SUPPORT OF LOVED ONES, YOU ARE NEVER ALONE. THEY HELP YOU FIND THE COURAGE TO MOVE ON IN LIFE.

MICHEL REVOY
I AM RETURNING TO THE SEA, WHERE MY PASSION LIES, AND WILL BE SURROUNDED BY THE ONES THAT I LOVE.
THAT IS WHERE HOME IS.
THAT IS WHERE I BELONG.

I HOPE TO RETURN WITH NEW DISCOVERIES AND NEW STORIES TO SHARE WITH YOU.

MEETING
COORDINATES
74° 41' 24.0" S
52° 05' 16.3" W

THIS IS DR. PAUL REVOY
SIGNING OFF...

AND ALWAYS REMEMBER...

A

FAMILY COMES FIRST.
MIETTE

When I originally pitched *The Aquanaut* to my publisher, the simple premise was, "sea creatures that convert an old diving suit into a land walking device to find a paradise on land to escape all the dangers of the sea." But as the story evolved, it became much more heartfelt. *The Aquanaut* became a story about loss, preserving legacies, family, and holding on to memories. Ten years later, while wrapping up the final parts of this book, my own father lost his battle to liver cancer, and I suddenly found myself feeling all the feelings that these characters were experiencing in the story, and the project became even more personal.

The following images are development pieces that I had sketched early on with some notes that you may find interesting.

Hope you enjoyed the journey as much as I enjoyed making it.

Dan Santat

EARLY DEVELOPMENT AQUANAUT DIVING SUIT

PAUL REVOY

Paul and Michel (pronounced Me-Shell) were both inspired by Jacques Cousteau and his marine research crew, who often wore iconic red wool beanies. I was always fascinated by old diving suits, and I was amused by the idea that sea creatures would attempt to use one as a fake human in an attempt to blend in with life on land, which I called "space" (the absence of water). In one scene that was deleted, I drew the sea creatures repurposing parts from a deep-diving submarine with robotic arms to build the Aquanaut.

The names of the sea characters were also indicative of the backstory of Sophia's mother. In the second panel on page 56 you see a woman in the family photos. This was Sophia's mother, and as you can see, she was a singer, inspired by my love of the Brazilian singer, Astrud Gilberto. The names of Sodapop's three crew members, Antonio, Carlos, and Jobim (pronounced "Joe-Beam"), are named after the famous Brazilian composer Antônio Carlos Jobim who, along with Astrud Gilberto, created hit songs, such as "The Girl From Ipanema." Their names give a glimpse into the mind of Sophia's father, Michel, who named these exotic sea creatures as a way to memorialize his wife.

SODAPOP

SOPHIA

CARLOS is the engineer of the crew, the one who operates the guts of the Aquanaut, and can multitask with all his limbs. I loved the idea that the crew consisted of all these rare and endangered sea creatures in search of others like themselves, who then realized that all the friends surrounding them were, in fact, their own adopted family.

ANTONIO is unique in the fact that a male Blanket octopus is 10,000 times smaller than a female and is extremely rare to find in nature.

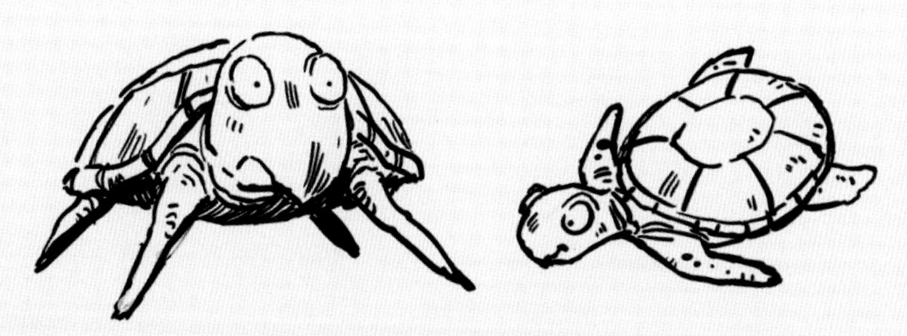

JOBIM, a Kemp's Ridley Sea Turtle, is the navigator of the bunch. He's more paternal than the rest in his instincts and keeps the crew in order. He's the Spock to Sodapop's Kirk.

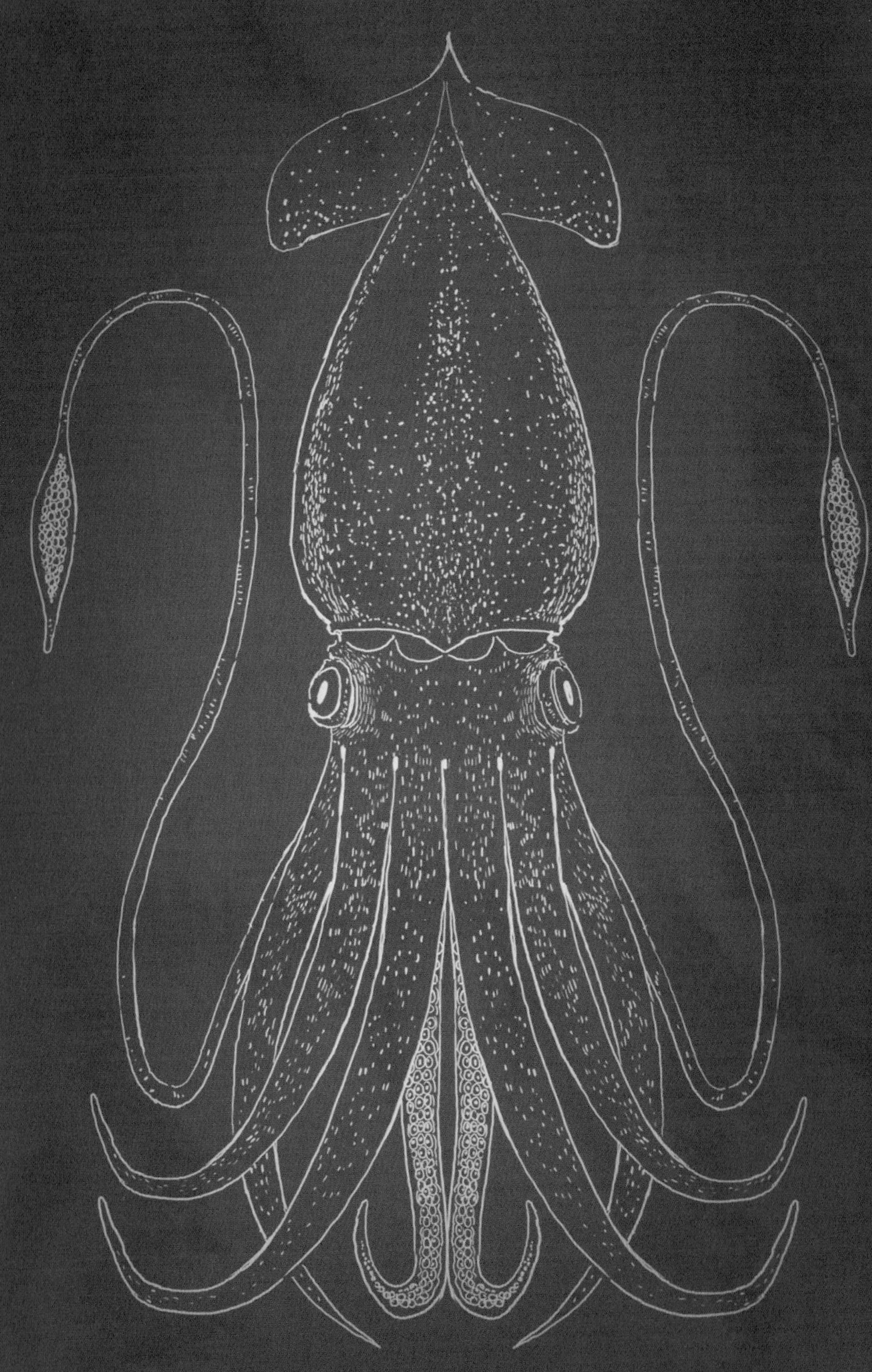

MESONYCHOTEUTHIS HAMILTONI

ACKNOWLEDGMENTS

The Aquanaut was a project that took over ten years to complete, to which there was no one to fault but myself, and within those years there are countless numbers of friends, family, and colleagues to thank.

Rachel Griffiths was the first editor of this book, and she waited patiently for five years for me to send her revisions while I was busy with a new family, a new home, and was juggling various other projects while setting my own off to the side.

Kait Feldmann was my second editor on this project, and for a year and a half she helped tighten up the story before she left to pursue greater heights in the publishing world.

David Saylor, the head of the Graphix imprint, helped finish the edits and kept the ship on the path toward completion.

Phil Falco, my art director, designer, and friend. You have always been my rock.

Mike Boldt, for coloring this book, and for his long-lasting friendship.

My friend, Arthur Levine, for giving me my big break in publishing and believing in this project.

My family, Leah, Alek, and Kyle for being my inspiration.

My agent, Jodi Reamer, for comforting me and telling me this book will be done when it's done.

And lastly, all my friends in the PBG. Renee, James, Ryan, Mike, Matt, Brett, Russ, Jess, Cale, and whoever decided to drop in on Skype.

Without all of you, this project would not have been possible. Without you I am nothing. You are all my family.

And family comes first.

DAN SANTAT is a #1 *New York Times* bestselling author/illustrator of over one hundred titles, which include *The Adventures of Beekle: The Unimaginary Friend*, the winner of the prestigious Randolph Caldecott Medal in 2015. Other titles include *Are We There Yet?*, *After the Fall (How Humpty Dumpty Got Back Up Again)*, and *Oh No! (Or How My Science Project Destroyed the World)*, which won the Silver Medal in book illustration from the Society of Illustrators in 2010. His first graphic novel, *Sidekicks*, was published by Scholastic/Graphix in 2011. He is also the creator of the Disney animated hit *The Replacements*.

Dan lives in Southern California with his wife, two kids, and various pets.

Visit him at beekleandfriends.com.

SIDEKICKS
DAN SANTAT
WINNER OF THE CALDECOTT MEDAL
USA

Captain Amazing, hero of Metro City, is so busy catching criminals that he rarely has time for his pets at home. He doesn't even notice when they develop superpowers of their own.

So when he announces that he needs a sidekick, his dog, hamster, and chameleon decide to audition. But with each pet determined to win the sidekick position, the biggest battle in Metro City might just be at the Captain's house.

Then archvillain Dr. Havoc returns to town, and suddenly the Captain's in serious trouble. Can the warring pets put their squabbles aside? Or is it curtains for the Captain?

It's sit, stay, and save the world in this romp of a graphic novel by Dan Santat!

SIDEKICKS

"Hilarious and heartfelt . . . a charming and well-told tale about friendship."
Kazu Kibuishi, creator of Amulet

"Lots of laughs and a boisterous and exuberant storyline."
Kirkus Reviews

"Lively, insightful, and just plain fun."
Bulletin of the Center for Children's Books

Library of Congress Control Number: 2021937540

ISBN 978-0-545-49760-2 (hardcover)
ISBN 978-0-545-49761-9 (paperback)

10 9 8 7 6 5 4 3 23 24 25 26

Printed in China 62
First edition, March 2022

Edited by Rachel Griffiths and Kait Feldmann
Book design by Steve Ponzo
Creative Director: Phil Falco
Publisher: David Saylor